more . . .

P9-DYB-724

ACCLAIM FOR
YOU'VE BEEN WARNED

"PATTERON'S VERSATILITY AND TALENT FOR HORROR—ABLY SUPPORTED BY HOWARD ROUGHAN'S OWN SKILLS ON THE DARK SIDE—ARE SHOWCASED IN *YOU'VE BEEN WARNED*. Readers are pulled through the novel by Kristin's vulnerable appeal, and by curiosity about how it's all going to end—and they won't be disappointed."
>—**BookLoons.com**

"FASCINATING AND INTRIGUING . . . Patterson's latest thriller draws the reader in with its unique plot."
>—**MysteryCrimeFiction.suite101.com**

"PACKS A LOT OF PUNCH! I actually had to read the last page twice . . . Enjoy this book!"
>—**MemphisReads.blogspot.com**

"PART MYSTERY, PART EROTICA, AND PART THRILLER, this is a Patterson novel with something for everyone."
>—**BookReporter.com**

"PATTERSON IS A MASTER."
>—*Toronto Globe and Mail*

Please turn this page for more reviews and turn to the back of this novel for a preview of James Patterson's new book, *Against Medical Advice*.

YOU'VE BEEN WARNED

ALSO BY JAMES PATTERSON

A complete list of books by James Patterson is on page 358-359.
For more information about James Patterson, go to
www.jamespatterson.com.

JAMES PATTERSON
& HOWARD ROUGHAN

YOU'VE BEEN
WARNED

GdC

GRAND CENTRAL
PUBLISHING

NEW YORK   BOSTON

Copyright © 2007 by James Patterson
Excerpt from *Against Medical Advice* copyright © 2008 by James Patterson. All rights reserved. Except as permitted under the U.S. Copyright Act of 1976, no part of this publication may be reproduced, distributed, or transmitted in any form or by any means, or stored in a database or retrieval system, without the prior written permission of the publisher.

Grand Central Publishing
Hachette Book Group USA
237 Park Avenue
New York, NY 10017
Visit our Web site at www.HachetteBookGroupUSA.com

Grand Central Publishing is a division of Hachette Book Group USA, Inc. The Grand Central Publishing name and logo is a trademark of Hachette Book Group USA, Inc.

Printed in the United States of America

Originally published in hardcover by Little, Brown and Company
First trade paperback edition: September 2007
First U.S. mass market edition: August 2008
First International mass market edition: August 2008

10 9 8 7 6 5 4 3 2 1

Character, like a photograph,
develops in darkness.

—Yousuf Karsh

YOU'VE BEEN
WARNED

Chapter 1

IT'S WAY TOO EARLY in the morning for dead people.

That's what I'd be thinking, were I actually thinking clearly right now. I'm not.

The second I turn the corner on my way to work and see the crowd, the commotion, the dingy gray body bags being wheeled out of that oh-so-chichi hotel, I reach for my camera. I can't help it. It's instinct on my part.

Click, click, click.

Don't think about what's happened here. Just shoot, Kristin.

My head whips left and right, the lens of my Leica R9 leading the way. I focus first on the faces around me — the gawkers, the lookie-loos. *That's what Annie Leibovitz would do.* A businessman in wide pinstripes, a bike messenger, a mother with her stroller, they all stand and stare at the terrible murder scene. Like it or not, this is the highlight of their day. And it's not yet eight a.m.

I move forward, even as something inside me is saying, "Look away, walk away." Even as something says, "You know where you are. This hotel. You know, Kristin."

I'm weaving my way toward the entrance to the hotel. Closer and closer, I'm being pulled—as if by an undertow that I can't resist. And I keep shooting pictures as though I'm on assignment for the *New York Times* or *Newsweek*.

Click, click, click.

Parked at jagged angles, police cars and ambulances fill the street. I look up from their sirens, tracing the twirling beams of blue-and-red light as they dance against the surrounding brownstones.

I spy more gawkers in the windows of nearby apartments. A woman wearing curlers takes a bite of a bagel. *Click.*

Something catches my eye. It's a reflection, the sun bouncing off the rail of the last gurney being wheeled out of the hotel. That makes four. *What happened in there? Murder? Mass murder?*

They sit, gathered on the sidewalk—four gurneys—each holding a body bag. It's horrifying. Just awful.

My wrist twists, and I go wide-angle to shoot them as a group—like a family. My wrist twists back, and I go tight, shooting them one by one. *Who were they? What happened to these poor people? How did they die?*

Don't think, Kristin, just shoot.

Two muscular paramedics walk out of the hotel and approach a couple of cops. Detectives, like on *Law & Order*. They all talk, they all shake their heads, and they all have that hardened New York look to them, as if they've seen it all before.

One of the detectives—older, rail thin—looks my way. I think he sees me.

Click, click, click.

Having burned through a roll of film, I furiously load another.

There's really nothing more to shoot, and yet I keep firing away. I'm late for work, but it doesn't matter. It's as if I can't leave.

Wait!

My head snaps back to the gurneys as something catches my eye. At first, I can't believe it. Maybe it's the wind, or just my mind playing tricks early in the morning.

Then it happens again, and I gasp. The last body bag . . . *it moved!*

Did I just see what I think I saw?

I'm terrified and want to run away. Instead, I edge even closer. Instinct? Undertow?

I'm staring at that zipped-up body bag, and all I know is that there's been a horrible mistake by the police or the EMS.

The zipper!

It's creeping backward. *That body bag is opening from the inside!*

My eyes bulge, and my knees buckle. Literally. I stagger through the crowd, staring through my lens in shock and disbelief.

I see a finger emerge, then an entire hand. *Oh, God, and there's blood!*

"Help!" I scream, lowering my camera. "That person is alive!"

The crowd turns, the cops and paramedics too. They glance at me and scoff in disbelief or reproach, shaking their heads as if I just escaped from Bellevue. *They think I'm nuts!*

I stab the air, pointing at the body bag as the hand pushes through the plastic, desperately reaching out for help. I think it's a woman's hand.

Do something, Kris! You have to save her!

I raise my camera again, and —

Chapter 2

I JOLT UP SO FAST I nearly break my neck. I'm drenched with sweat, crying hysterically, and have no idea where I am. Everything is blurry, so I try to rub my eyes into focus, but it's hard because my hands are trembling out of control. Actually, my whole body is trembling.

I plead with myself, *C'mon, Kris*.

Finally, shapes begin to appear before me, followed by outlines . . . and, like a Polaroid, it all becomes clear.

It was just a dream, you spaz! Just a dream.

Collapsing back into my pillow, I let out the world's hugest sigh of relief. Never have I been so happy to be alone in my own bed.

But it was so real.

The body bags . . . a woman's hand coming out of one of them.

I turn to my alarm clock—a little before six a.m. Good, I can still get a few more minutes of sleep. But the moment I close my eyes, they pop right open again.

I hear something, a pounding, and it's not just my stressed-out heart. Someone's at the door.

Throwing on the same blue terry cloth robe I've had since my Boston College days, I trudge across my tiny apartment, which is decorated with the very finest furnishings from the Crate & Barrel factory-reject sale. So what if my couch has only three legs and belongs in a Farrelly brothers movie?

The pounding gets louder. More urgent and annoying. *All right already, hold your horses!*

Approaching the door, I don't call out and ask who it is. That's what peepholes are for, especially in Manhattan.

Quietly, I lean forward and squint to look with a tired eye.

Shit.

Her.

I open the door. Glaring at me through a pair of drugstore bifocals is my nosy old neighbor from down the hall, Mrs. Rosencrantz. She's clearly ticked off about something, and that makes two of us.

"Do you realize what time it is?" I grumble.

"Do *you* realize what time it is?" she shoots back. "Once and for all, you've got to stop this psychotic screaming every morning."

I look at Mrs. Rosencrantz—all four feet ten of her—as if she's the one who's psychotic. I may have been crying, but I certainly wasn't *screaming*.

"You know, if you really want to hassle someone about noise, Mrs. Rosencrantz, you should find out who's playing that music at six a.m."

She gives me a sideways look. "What music?"

"C'mon, you don't hear that? It's coming from . . ." I step into the hallway, turning my head left and right.

Wait—where exactly is it coming from?

Mrs. Rosencrantz shakes her head and huffs. "I don't hear any music, Ms. Burns. And if you're trying to be a little smart-ass with me, I'm telling you right now I don't appreciate it."

"Mrs. Rosencrantz, I'm not trying to —"

She cuts me off. "Don't think I can't get you evicted, because I can."

I frown at the old bat, who happens to look even more unpleasant and haggard than usual, if that's possible. *You want smart-ass, lady? I'll give you smart-ass!*

"Mrs. Rosencrantz, I'm going back to bed now . . . and if you don't mind my saying so, you could use a little more beauty sleep yourself."

With that, I promptly close the door on her stunned, sourpuss face.

I'm about to turn and make a beeline for my bed, when I catch a glimpse of myself in the mirror by the coat closet. *Whoa!* I'm sporting some serious raccoon eyes and a pretty spectacular case of bedhead. *Omigod, I look almost as bad as Mrs. Rosencrantz!*

Supposedly, I have this killer wink that everybody loves. I wink at myself in the mirror. It doesn't help. I wink at myself again. Nope, nothing.

I laugh out loud, and for a moment, I forget about the horrible dream and my neighbor from hell.

But only for a moment.

Because I still can't figure out the music and where it's coming from.

Walking around my apartment like Elmer Fudd hunting rabbits, I press my ear against the walls. Feeling totally ridiculous, I drop to my knees and try listening through the floorboards.

Only after grabbing a chair to climb closer to the ceiling do I realize what's going on. The music isn't *coming* from anywhere.

The music is inside my head.

Chapter 3

THIS IS NOT GOOD!

I stand perfectly still in my living room and try to listen . . . *between my ears.* The music is faint, but it's definitely there. *How bizarre is this? How scary? What a weird, weird morning this has been, and I've barely been out of bed five minutes.*

I close my eyes. It's a song, and it sounds familiar. I've definitely heard it before. For the life of me, though, I can't put my finger on it.

Just keep quiet and keep listening, I tell myself.

But in the next second, I can do neither, as the silence in my apartment is upended by the phone ringing. It's okay, though. *It's always okay when he calls.*

"Hello?"

"Good morning, sweetheart," Michael whispers, "this is your phone sex wake-up call."

I've heard him say the line a hundred times and still I giggle. "Good morning," I whisper back. And now I'm smiling.

"How did you sleep, Kris?"

"Don't ask."

"Why? What's wrong?"

"I had this horrible, horrible dream, and to top it off, my crackpot neighbor just pounded on my door and flipped out on me."

"Let me guess," he says. "It's that nasty old lady from down the hall. The one out of *Rosemary's Baby*."

"Bingo. The woman's got one foot in the grave and the other in her mouth. I swear, the things she says, she's going to drive me crazy." *Maybe she has already.*

"Even more of a reason to move, Kris."

"I knew you were going to say that."

"The offer still stands. It's only what you deserve."

"I told you, Michael, I don't want you getting me a new place. I need to do it myself. I will. My portfolio is at the Abbott Show. I'm gonna be a star. *Aren't* I?"

"Of course you are. But you're so stubborn sometimes."

"That's what you love about me."

"You're right," he says. "The fact that you're smart, talented, and gorgeous has nothing to do with it."

God, how I love him. *He's such a sweetheart!*

Mind you, it doesn't hurt that he's also handsome, athletic, and a managing partner at Baer Stevens Asset Management. Michael could buy me *ten* new apartments without batting an eyelash.

"So, are you already at the office?" I ask.

"Of course. Either you eat the Baer Stevens, or the Baer Stevens —"

I chuckle. The sun's barely up. "I don't know how you do it."

"Clean living, that's how."

"Ha."

"Speaking of *doing it,* though . . ."

"Very funny, lover boy. Just for that you're going to have to buy me dinner first."

"Damn, I wish I could, except I've got to wine and dine some important clients in town for the night. Business before pleasure, as they say. What about *after* dinner? You could be my dessert. *Yum.*"

"We'll just see about yum."

Of course, Michael knows that's as good as a yes with me. All I really want to do is my photography and be with him, my *almost* perfect man.

"Now tell me," I say.

His voice drops to a whisper again. "I love you, Kristin. I adore you. I can't live without you."

"And I love you, et cetera, et cetera, et cetera. I do, Michael."

He sighs. "Such music to my ears. You really do love me, don't you?"

I don't respond. I can't. The word has me momentarily frozen.

Music.

It dawns on me that since Michael called, I no longer hear the song in my head. *What a relief!* I'm not losing my mind after all.

"Kristin, you there?" he asks.

For a split second, I consider telling him about the music. I don't, though. It's a little too flaky.

"Yeah, I'm here," I say.

"You okay?"

"I'm fine—sorry, I was just checking the time. Don't want to be late for work."

"You're right," he says. "I'll let you go. Lord knows you don't want to piss off that boss of yours."

Chapter 4

SO, WHAT OTHER BAD THING can possibly happen to me this morning?

I think I'm kidding as I hang up and head for the bathroom. That's when I turn on the shower and discover there's no hot water. *Ugh! No way!*

Now there's a different sound in my head. It's Michael, laughing, with yet another reason why I should let him be my sugar daddy and buy me an apartment. *No way!*

Shivering under what amounts to an arctic drizzle, I proceed to take the world's fastest shower.

I dress, gulp some OJ while munching on a Chai Tea Luna bar, and do a quick inventory of my shoulder bag before heading out the door. It's all there — wallet, keys, cell phone, and the only other thing I carry with me at all times, my Leica.

Walking up Second Avenue past 46th Street, I pass the same cramped newsstand I do every day. It's lined sidewalk to ceiling with every magazine imaginable, and I glance at the covers, my eyes taking in the flawless faces of various celebrities and supermodels. *Good morning, Brad, Leo, Gisele, Angelina.*

Funny, most people want to *be* them. I just want to photograph them.

That's my dream, and I'm getting very close, according to my agent and a few big editors. And hopefully according to the Abbott Show, the prestige gallery where my work is being considered. But until it comes true—when I make a name for myself and those same famous people shout, "Get me Kristin Burns!" for the cover of *Vanity Fair*—I keep right on walking.

To my job as a nanny.

Cutting over to Third Avenue, I head up five blocks before crossing to Lexington. I head north five more blocks and then cut across again, to Park Avenue. I do the same thing every day, the same zigzag pattern. Don't know why—I just do. Or maybe I do know why, and do it anyway.

Normally, I'd be taking pictures along the way, capturing the faces of the drones as they head to work while trying not to dwell on the fact that I'm one of them. There's not a lot of happiness along the sidewalks at this early hour. What I see is fatigue, angst, and a tremendous amount of boredom.

Of course, that's what makes for good photographs. I mean, when's the last time a smile won the Pulitzer?

Still, after the morning I've had, I decide to keep the camera tucked away in my shoulder bag. I'm feeling a little preoccupied. I'd say my head is in the clouds, except there aren't any today. It's a beautiful blue-skied morning in the middle of May, the kind of day that makes people happy to be alive.

So I take a deep breath and berate myself. *Snap out of it, Kristin!* And for a while, I do.

Right up until I turn the corner onto Madison.

And scream.

Not just a little one either.

I scream at the top of my lungs.

Chapter 5

OMIGOD. Omigod.

The police cars, the ambulances, the twirling beams of blue and red light.

This can't be happening. It isn't possible. . . . But there it is anyway. Plus an awful smell in the air — like something burning!

The crowd gathered in front of the same hotel and the gurneys being wheeled out the entrance.

Can't be! Cannot!

But it is.

My dream . . . *it's happening!*

Everything just as I saw it. Every person too — the pin-striped businessman, the bike messenger, the mother with her stroller — all watching the murder scene.

And that smell — that's new — but what is it?

I close my eyes, squeezing them tight as if to reboot my brain. *Am I really seeing this?*

Yes. I am seeing this, every insane detail.

My eyes blink open, and I'm still standing on the

corner of 68th and Madison, in front of the Fálcon Hotel.
The Fálcon, of all places.

I want to run away. I know I should bolt while the
bolting's good. Instead, I reach for my camera.

Don't think, just shoot.

But I *am* thinking.

As my finger clicks madly away, I'm thinking that this
is impossible, that it can't be real, and the more I think
this, the more I know I have to keep shooting.

I need proof.

The same powerful undertow as the one in my dream
grabs hold of me as I inch closer to the entrance of the
Fálcon. I look up at the windows of the surrounding
brownstones and see the woman in curlers taking a bite
out of her bagel.

Click, click, click.

My heart is pounding, pounding, pounding, as if
there's a big bass drum inside my chest.

I look at my hands. Then at my arms. There's a rash all
over me—or maybe it's hives.

Suddenly, I can't breathe. The final body is being
wheeled out of the hotel, and this is the last chance for
me to run away.

I don't run.

My feet don't move, and my camera lens is fixed on
the four gurneys gathered on the sidewalk. I'm gasping
for air, drowning in my own fear, just about to lose it
big-time.

Because I know what happens next.

"Help!" I yell out.

The mere thought of the zipper moving on that body

bag is enough. I don't need to wait to see it happen. Once was plenty.

I lower my camera and frantically wave my arms.

"Help!" I yell again, much louder this time. "Please, help!"

I'm shaking as I start to cry, the tears streaming down my cheeks. The rash, the hives—it's getting worse.

This is unbearable.

"Please, someone, listen to me."

And that's when someone does.

Chapter 6

I SEE HIS EYES FIRST, very dark, intense, and unblinking, staring right into mine.

He's dressed in a gray suit, nothing fancy, jacket open with a loose tie, yellow-and-red stripe. Clipped to his belt is a scuffed-up badge. *NYPD?*

With a deliberate gait bordering on slow, he weaves his way through the crowd and walks up to me. All this time, his eyes never leave mine. I guess he heard me screaming. I smell his aftershave . . . and tobacco.

"Oh, thank God," I say, a relieved hand slapping my chest. "Are you with the police?"

"I'm a detective, yes."

I point back at the hotel. "Hurry, you have to do something."

He gives me a strange look before glancing over his shoulder. "Excuse me? I have to do *what?*"

I jab my finger at the gurneys again, the words tripping over my tongue. "The zipper . . . over there . . . the one on the . . ." I take a deep breath and spit it out. "The person in that last body bag is still alive!"

The detective looks at the hotel again. It's not quite a smirk on his hardened face when he turns back to me, but it's close. There is something unsettling about this man, deeply so.

"Lady, I can assure you the person in that bag is dead. They're *all* dead."

"Please, just go check."

He shakes his head. "No, I won't go check. Did you hear what I just told you?"

"You don't understand, Detective. The zipper on that last body bag, it's going to—"

I stop myself cold. *Hold it right there, Kris. Not another word!*

I complete the sentence in my head and suddenly, embarrassingly, I realize how crazy it all sounds. I sneak a quick peek at that last body bag, which still hasn't moved. I want to tell this guy about the dream; I want to make him believe me.

So of course I *can't* tell him about the dream.

"I'm sorry," I say meekly, starting to put away my camera. "I don't know what I was thinking. I guess I just got scared."

"Four murders," he says. "That's scary, all right."

I can feel the detective's eyes on me as I fumble with the lens cap for my camera, but I don't look at him. And as I turn to slink away as quickly as possible, I don't say another word. No good-bye, no apology, no nothing. *Way to go, Kristin. You've just made a complete fool of yourself.*

It's been a morning to remember.

Four dead bodies.

Déjà dead?

Whatever.

Chapter 7

THE RASH, whatever it was, is gone now. So is that awful burning smell. *Why was that different than in my dream?*

Thankfully, I'm not very good at running and *dwelling,* otherwise I'd be obsessing about what did or didn't just happen as I race up to the Turnbulls' building on Fifth Avenue across from Central Park.

For now, what I force myself to think about is that I'm late for work and how that's a major no-no with the boss, something Louis, the morning doorman for the building, is all too pleased to point out as I blow by him.

"Uh-oh," he says, slowly shaking his nearly bald head. "Somebody's in trouble. Never let 'em see you sweat, Miss Kristin."

"Good morning to you too, Louis," I say over my shoulder.

"Overslept, huh?"

If only.

I hop on the elevator and press PH for the penthouse, the top, the ritz.

Eighteen stories later, I step out onto the black-and-white-checked marble of the foyer that separates the only two apartments on the floor. My rushed footsteps echo as I steer left to the Turnbull residence with key in hand.

Please let her be in a good mood.

Fat chance.

Opening the door, I see Penley's rail-thin frame standing before me. It doesn't matter how much Restylane she's got spackling her frown lines, I can tell she's pissed.

"You're late," she announces, her voice detached and chilly.

"I know, I'm sorry. I'm really sorry."

"Sorry doesn't work for me, Kristin." She picks a piece of lint from her designer workout clothes. Nearly every morning, she heads to the gym after I arrive. "You know I have to be able to rely on you," she says.

"Yes, I know."

"From where I'm standing, I'm not so sure you do. In fact, I'm pretty sure that you don't."

I look at Penley "the Pencil" Turnbull and want to scream so loud it will break crystal, and there's plenty of it in earshot. Her patronizing tone, the way she refuses to yell at me because that would be *sooo* middle-class, it drives me absolutely bonkers.

Penley folds her arms. It's her Mommie Dearest pose. Actually, her *Step*mommie Dearest pose. "So, can I still rely on you, Kristin?"

"Yes, of course you can."

"Good. I'm glad we've had this little talk."

She begins to walk away, then stops, very nearly pirouettes. Almost as an afterthought, she updates me on the kids, of whom she isn't the natural mother. Their real mother died in a shooting accident the year Sean was born.

"Dakota and Sean are both in the kitchen, finishing their breakfast. Oh, and be sure to double-check that they have everything for school. I don't want to get another note home saying they forgot something. It's *embarrassing*."

Yes, Your Highness.

I watch Penley glide down the hallway to her bedroom before I start for the kitchen. I only get a few steps when the phone rings. I pick it up in the study.

"Hello, Turnbull residence."

"Is the boss in the room?"

It's Michael.

I lower my voice. "No. You just missed the mistress."

"Were you late?"

"Yes."

"Was she a bitch to you?"

"You have to ask?"

"I guess you've got a point there," he says. "So, how are you, anyway?"

"Michael . . ."

"What?"

"What did I tell you about calling me here?"

"Who says I called for you?"

"Yeah, right, like you actually want to speak with Penley."

"What, a guy can't talk to his wife?"

"You know what I mean; it's risky."

"I keep telling you, Penley doesn't believe in answering the phone. That's what she has you for."

Right then, I hear a voice behind me. *Her* voice. "Who is that, Kristin?" asks Penley.

I nearly swallow my stomach.

"Oh, gosh, you startled me," I say, breathless.

She couldn't care less. "I asked who you were talking to."

"No one," I answer.

"It's obviously *someone*." She gives me a disapproving glare. "That's not a personal call, is it? Because you know how I feel about those when you're supposed to be working."

"No, it's not a personal call," I assure her. *Unless, of course, you count your husband.*

"Then who is it?"

I think fast. "It's some guy from Lincoln Center. He wants to know if you'd be interested in attending an opera series they're doing."

Penley cocks her head and shoots me a suspicious look.

So I gamble.

"Here," I say, offering her the phone. "You can talk to him if you want."

Penley — a devout macrobiotic dieter — looks at the phone as if it's a Twinkie. No, worse — a *fried* Twinkie. She wants nothing to do with any "salesman type," even one from Lincoln Center.

She sniffs. "I thought we were on that do-not-call list."

"You know, you're right," I say, relishing the thought of repeating this to Michael. He's undoubtedly been listening the entire time. "We are on that do-not-call list," I say into the phone.

Sure enough, as I hang up I can hear him laughing hysterically.

Michael Turnbull, my *almost* perfect man, loves to live on the edge. And he loves it even more when I join him there.

Chapter 8

I LOVE DAKOTA AND SEAN. Who wouldn't? That's the message lettered on T-shirts I gave the Turnbull kids last Christmas. It also happens to be absolutely true. I feel sorry for the kids because their stepmother is such an uncaring bitch toward them.

As we ride the elevator down to the lobby, Sean stares up at me with his big blue curious eyes. At age five, everything—and I mean *everything*—is a question for this darling little boy.

"Miss Kristin, how old are you?" he asks.

His sister, Dakota, seven going on seventeen, immediately chimes in. "You're not supposed to ask a woman how old she is, dummy!"

"That's okay, sweetheart. Sean can ask me anything." I flash him a reassuring smile. "I'm twenty-six."

He blinks his baby blues a few times as if mulling it over. "That's really old, isn't it?"

Dakota slaps her forehead. "Oh, brother! And I mean *brother.*"

I laugh—something I do a lot when it's just the three of us, especially during our daily trek to Preston Academy, or as *New York* magazine prefers, "The 'it' school for tykes on the Upper East Side that's harder to get into than Fort Knox."

"Miss Kristin, why do kids have to go to school?" asks Sean without missing a beat.

"That's easy. So they can learn lots of neat things and grow up to be really smart like their parents," I explain. "Isn't that right, Dakota?"

"I guess," she says with a shrug.

Sean blinks again. "Are you smart, Miss Kristin?"

"I like to think I am," I say.

Yet it's moments like this that make me wonder, and question myself. I care about these two kids so damn much and would never do anything to hurt them. So why am I having an affair with their father?

I know why.

I can't help myself.

Michael is wonderful, and he loves me, and I love him as much as we both do Dakota and Sean.

As for stepmom Penley, she treats the kids like fashion accessories, to be seen adoringly at her side like an Hermès or a Chanel bag. She doesn't make time for them as much as she allots it, scheduling the two children into her life the same way she does luncheons and museum committee meetings.

I hate the term *home wrecker,* and if for one moment I thought I was actually wrecking something wonderful, I'd be out of their lives in an instant. But I spend a lot of time in that penthouse apartment, and I see what's going on.

Yes, maybe my head knows better. In my heart, however, I'm convinced that the four of us—Dakota, Sean, Michael, and me—are destined to be together.

It's going to happen.

Soon.

Chapter 9

WE BOUND OFF the elevator and right into the playful smile of Louis. "Well, if it isn't the Three Musketeers!" he exclaims.

Louis reaches to the side of his doorman's coat and brandishes an imaginary sword. On cue, Sean goes for his. Their daily make-believe duel lasts all the way across the lobby.

It's always fun to watch, especially today. After the morning I've had, this ritual—this return to normalcy—is exactly what I need.

I laugh and cheer Sean on as Louis pretends to be fatally wounded. With all the gusto of a B movie actor, he drops to his knees and dies a slow, painful death.

Maybe that's what does it.

Or maybe it's simply being outside again.

Either way, no sooner do I set foot on the sidewalk than my thoughts return to the Fálcon Hotel and my dream—that horrible, horrible *dream*—coming to life.

Instantly, I'm awash in all the disturbing images again. They're vivid in my mind and at the same time confusing.

New Yorkers, more than anyone, don't like things they can't rationally explain. That goes for nonnative New Yorkers as well. Like me.

"Miss Kristin, is everything okay?"

It's not Sean asking the question this time, it's Dakota. Not only is she mature for her age, I think she's also a mind reader.

"Everything's fine, sweetheart. Why do you ask?"

"Because you're squeezing extra tight this morning."

I look down and, sure enough, I can see the white of my knuckles wrapped around her tiny hand. Same for the one around Sean's.

"I'm sorry," I say, loosening my grip. "I guess I like holding on to you both so much, I never want to let go."

"Fine with me," says Sean blithely.

We continue walking, and I struggle to clear my mind of all the bad images from earlier. It's near impossible. A howling ambulance passes us on the street, and it's as if I'm seeing it all yet again. The body bags, the zipper . . .

The woman's hand covered with blood.

"Miss Kristin, you're doing it again," says Dakota, trying to wiggle her fingers free.

"Yeah," says Sean. "You're like my G.I. Joe with kung fu grip!"

A few minutes later we arrive at Madison and 74th, and the imposing wrought-iron gates of the Preston Academy. I kneel to kiss Sean and Dakota good-bye.

"Have a great day, my angels."

"You too, Miss Kristin," chirps Sean. "Have a great day."

Dakota peers into my eyes. "Are you sure everything's okay?"

"I'm sure," I answer.

But of course I'm not.

Then I wink at the kids, and they wink back. They have killer winks too.

I stand there and watch the kids dash off, joining their classmates marching up the steps to the school. They look so happy, so carefree.

So innocent.

Chapter 10

THE TWO BEST THINGS about my job disappear through the front door of Preston Academy, and I'm left walking back to the worst thing.

Penley.

That and what she likes to call "light housekeeping," or sometimes "chores."

While the kids are at school, Penley keeps me busy with . . . well . . . *busy*work. Let's just say the woman is extremely anal-retentive. Last week, while having me organize the pantry, she insisted I arrange the cans of soup in alphabetical order.

As for the "heavy housekeeping"—changing the bed linens, washing and ironing, cleaning the bathrooms, et cetera—that's taken care of by Maria, the twice-a-week maid. I think she's great. Originally from Morelia, Mexico, she's an incredibly hard worker and boasts a wonderful smile. As for how she manages to put up with Penley and her biting tongue, I can only attribute it to Maria's very limited grasp of the English language.

I, on the other hand, can understand perfectly all the

ridiculously demeaning things that Penley says to me on a daily basis.

So rushing back to that penthouse apartment after dropping off Dakota and Sean holds little appeal. I prefer to take my time, today being no exception. Since I haven't been able to make any sense of what happened, or seemed to happen, earlier, I'm trying to keep my thoughts on anything but.

I stroll south on Madison Avenue. The sunlight is perfect, and the urge to snap some pictures returns. I reach for my camera and automatically I'm excited.

As I take off the lens cap, I can't help thinking about Michael. When he's not trying to put me into a nicer apartment, he's offering to jump-start my career by financing my own gallery or getting me a prestige magazine shoot.

But I won't let him do that. None of it.

It's important to me that I do this on my own, even if that means barely scraping by, living paycheck to paycheck. I'm not a *complete* fool, mind you—Michael is allowed to take me out, buy me dinners and other fun stuff—but I never want to feel as if I'm beholden to him. And deep down, though he'll never admit it, I think he doesn't want me to feel that way either. That's another reason I love him. I do. I do.

I keep looking for more great shots to build my portfolio, clicking away when I'm lucky enough to see them. And today—*yeah!*—I'm seeing them.

A little farther down Madison, I spot a man in a skullcap, washing the front window of a restaurant, his disgruntled reflection crystal clear in the wake of his squeegee.

It creates a fantastic double image of working-class

angst, and I shoot it from a couple of angles, commiserating with the guy.

Then I pass a woman smoking a cigarette outside a Coach leather store. She's undoubtedly a sales clerk on break, the hunched posture and faraway gaze providing more than enough proof. I take two shots, one of her and one of her shadow.

I smile behind my lens. *This is really good stuff!*

So good in fact that I lose track of how far I've walked.

Before I know it, I'm standing less than a block away from the Fálcon.

That was a close one, I tell myself. Surely the only thing worse than returning to work would be facing that hotel again. Especially since the Fálcon and I have some history anyway. To put it mildly.

So why aren't my feet moving?

All I have to do is turn around and head up and over to Fifth Avenue. Easy as pumpkin pie.

And yet I don't. It's as if that powerful undertow has taken hold of me again, fighting my urge to walk away.

What, are you nuts, Kristin?

No, I'm not. I'm one of the sanest people I know. That's what makes all of this so strange.

Inexplicably, I feel drawn to the Fálcon and what happened there this morning.

What did happen there?

I don't know, do I? Not really.

I need to watch the news. I need to develop the pictures too. But first I need to do something else.

Walk away.

Quickly, I do just that.

See? I'm back in control.

Chapter 11

I RUSH THROUGH the door of my apartment at a few minutes after five that night.

I should be exhausted. Penley had me polish every piece of silverware for sixteen place settings, including not one, not two, but three different-sized salad forks. *Three,* for crying out loud!

And as she occasionally peered over my shoulder to make sure I didn't miss a spot, I fantasized about stabbing her with all of them.

On the bright side — *always* on the bright side — were Dakota and Sean. After I picked up my little sweethearts from school in the afternoon, we walked to Central Park and played tag and "nanny in the middle" in the Sheep Meadow for over an hour.

Like I said, I should be exhausted.

But I'm not. I'm too anxious to be tired, too tense. I'm dying to find out what happened at the Fálcon Hotel this morning. I need to have this strange mystery solved.

I put down my bag, kick off my flats, and grab a Vitamin Water from the fridge — the peach-mango flavor, a personal favorite. Then I head straight for the TV and the start of the first "Live at Five" news program I can find.

"Good afternoon, here's what's happening . . . ," begins the perfectly coiffed male anchor. *Seriously, it looks as if he's wearing a hair helmet.*

He and his female cohort take turns reading "the top stories of the day." A water main break in the Flatbush section of Brooklyn. Yet another fatal stabbing in Queens. A taxi that jumped the curb down on Wall Street and collided with the cart of one very angry hot-dog vendor.

But nothing about the Fálcon.

How could that be?

If a runaway cab taking out a bunch of hot dogs is considered newsworthy, certainly the death of four people at a hotel in Midtown is as well.

Or is it already old news? Maybe what I saw this morning was the lead story for the noontime broadcast and now they've moved on to other tales of woe. It is a big city, after all. Plenty of mayhem and misery to go around.

I flip the channel.

Another anchor duo appears, but it's the same result, nothing about any "tragedy" at the Fálcon. Maybe they had it as one of their top stories and I missed it.

Or maybe I just imagined the whole thing. *This is getting really creepy.*

The dream was a real dream, but what I saw on the way to work was a figment of my imagination? A physical manifestation of my emotional distress, as my ex-shrink, Dr. Corey, might say. *Yeah, and in my spare time I'm Gwyneth Paltrow!*

I know what I saw and I know it happened on my way to work this morning. I was there! And should there be any doubt, I know just one thing to do.

I get up from the TV and head over to my shoulder bag. Reaching in, I grab my camera and the rolls of film I shot this morning.

It's time to hit the darkroom.

Chapter 12

I THINK OF IT as my home away from home—never mind that it happens to be *inside* my apartment. A converted walk-in closet, to be exact. Basically a shoe box.

I step in, close the door behind me, and take a long, deep, stress-releasing breath. *Hello, darkness, my old friend.*

After the creepy day I've had, it's strange that a narrow, claustrophobic room with black corkboard walls, no windows, and a mere seven watts of light makes me feel at peace.

But that's why I built this thing in the first place.

My darkroom.

My safe house.

Beyond the joy I derive from developing my own pictures—*Call me old-fashioned; no, call me a purist*—there's that wonderful feeling in the darkroom of being able to shut out the rest of the world and all the problems that go with it. *Problems—outside! Out!*

Inside here, it's strictly my photography and me.

Okay, let's do this. Let's get it over with. Let's see what's what.

I turn off my safelight and, in complete darkness, load the rolls of film onto developing reels. Everything is by touch, but I've done this so many times I don't even have to think about it.

With each reel secured in a small processing tank, I'm able to turn the safelight back on. A faint red glow fills the room immediately.

Time for the soup.

One by one, the magic ingredients get added to each tank. Chemical developer followed by water mixed with a pinch of acetic acid followed by a fixer.

If only I could cook like I develop film.

Now comes my usual moment of trepidation, when my heart flutters for a beat or two. It happens with every roll, and it's certainly happening with *these*.

As the negatives begin to harden, this is my first chance to see what I've got.

If anything, right?

I lean forward a bit and try to harness all seven watts of visibility in the room. The thought of having to relive that terrible scene at the hotel frame by frame makes me more than a little uneasy. But it's nothing compared to the thought of the shots' not being there at all.

In this case, I'll gladly take the lesser of two evils. Scary reality beats *no* reality.

Through my squinting eyes, the images begin to appear. Shot after shot of the scene, just as I saw it. *Just as it happened!*

I straighten up and exhale. I didn't expect to feel this

crazily relieved and yet I do. So much so, I almost don't see it.

There's something strange about these pictures.

The day's mystery continues, only it's getting worse.

And I think that burning smell is back too.

Chapter 13

I IMMEDIATELY PLUNGE the negatives into a holding bath of cold water. My nose practically takes a dip as I lean in for a closer look.

It's hard to tell exactly what's wrong with the shots, but something is. That burning smell has definitely returned. I look at my hands . . . no hives yet.

Amid the stark whites and recessed blacks of the film, there's something going on—some type of effect taking place.

What, though?

I yank the negatives from the water and grab my magnifying loupe, pressing my eye tight against it.

I study one shot and then slide the loupe to the next. I do this quickly, anxiously, over and over. Study . . . *slide* . . . study . . . *slide*.

Finally, I think I see what's happening. Or at least *where* it's happening.

It's the four body bags.

They look almost . . . *transparent.* Is that possible?

It's like I can both see the bags and almost see through them—not to what's inside, but to what's beyond.

Of course, the film itself is transparent, but this is different. Each body bag has this kind of lucent quality, not quite see-through while at the same time not entirely filled in.

Somewhere in between.

Weird.

Though explainable, right? My mind spins with the possible causes. Double exposure, sun glare off the metal frames of the gurneys, the body bag material itself. Within seconds, I have a host of somewhat logical explanations for what I see.

But no definitive answer, nothing that makes me feel the least bit better.

So, when in doubt, go big. That's what I'm thinking as I dispense with a contact sheet and delve right into making an enlargement.

Scanning the shots again, I pull the one with the tightest angle for the most detail.

It takes a few seconds before I realize which one I've chosen. Figures!

It's the last body bag that was wheeled out of the hotel, the one with the moving zipper and the—I don't even want to think about it.

Besides, that was only in the dream. This is real. This is happening right now, before my eyes.

I fumble with the negative carrier before putting it in the enlarger. I make sure the emulsion side is facing down so as not to get a mirror image. The last thing I need is *another* glitch!

I work fast. Impatience is such a great motivator. So is

fear. Before long I'm staring at an eight-by-ten enlargement of that last body bag. Everything's bigger, all right.

The problem is, I'm no closer to figuring out what in God's name is happening. The effect—the transparency—is unlike anything I've seen, and I've developed a whole lot of photographs in my life.

From the moment I awoke this morning until now, it's been one big weirdness-palooza. And I hate paloozas!

I glance at my watch. Almost 7:30. *Where did the time go?*

I decide to make more enlargements. Maybe another shot will reveal something. What I'm really doing, though, is trying to keep my mind off, well, everything that's happened so far today.

For a while it works. Then, after another hour, it gets the better of me. I leave the darkroom and begin pacing in my living room.

It's too early for bed. Besides, I'm too wired to sleep. *I need to get out of here!*

And I know just where to go.

Chapter 14

I STEP OUT OF THE CAB in front of the Old Homestead Steak House in the heart of the meatpacking district. As if the location alone isn't enough to scare off vegetarians, there's a humongous cow over the entrance. Very subtle.

Who am I to talk?

If there's a list of what never to do when you're having an affair, I'm pretty sure crashing your lover's business dinner is right up there at the top.

I walk into the restaurant and breeze by the maître d' as if I know where I'm going. I don't.

In front of me there's a crowded bar and an equally crowded lounge area, beyond which begins the crowded dining room. The way it's laid out, I can see only the first few tables.

As I make my way to a better view, one thing becomes clear. With its dark wood paneling, leather club chairs, and portions that could choke the Lincoln Tunnel, this is definitely a place for *guys*. In fact, there are very few gals to be seen.

"May I help you?"

The voice startles me. I turn around to see the maître d'. So much for blowing right by him.

"I'm just looking for someone," I say.

"Perhaps I can help you."

"No, that's okay."

He glances down at what I'm wearing—a black Elie Tahari waistcoat over jeans and an Armani Exchange sweater. Stylish, perhaps, but not exactly "female executive" attire.

"Really, I insist," he says.

I more than catch his drift. He's not *asking* if he can help me, he's telling me.

"In that case, his name is Michael Turnbull," I say. "He comes here fairly often."

"Yes, of course. Come this way; Mr. Turnbull's seated in the back with his guests."

I hesitate. "Actually, would you mind telling him that I'm here?"

"I see. And you are?"

Clearly not his wife.

"Kristin," I say.

There's an awkward silence between us.

"I'm his assistant," I tack on. Immediately I regret it.

The maître d' smiles—a little too knowingly—and disappears into the dining room.

Good one, Kris! Why not just grab a bullhorn and scream out, MISTRESS ALERT! MISTRESS ALERT!

I continue berating myself while I wait for Michael. All I can hope is that he'll be more surprised than angry and not the other way around.

But it's not Michael who appears from the dining room a few moments later.

It's the maître d' again.

Chapter 15

"HE *WHAT?*"

"Mr. Turnbull asked that you join him at his table," repeats the maître d'.

I look at the guy so sideways I nearly lose my balance. "Are you sure about that?"

"Very."

The next thing I know I'm being led to the back of the dining room. It dawns on me. *This is sooo Michael.*

So confident. So in control.

So much why I love him.

It's no surprise he runs such a successful hedge fund. He never met a risk he couldn't minimize.

"Ah, there she is!" he says.

It's a large round table and yet there's little doubt as to who's sitting at the head. Michael stands up from his chair, flashing his killer smile. As he walks over to me, wineglass in hand, he throws the maître d' a quick wink as if to say, *I'll take it from here.*

He certainly does.

"Kristin, come meet my friends from the Royal Queen

Bank of Sweden." Michael turns to the table and actually puts his arm around me. "Gentlemen!" he announces. "Jag vill att ni alla möter min sekreterare, Kristin."

I blush slightly as the entire group—all men and each blonder than the next—proceeds to raise wineglasses and smile. They don't look like bankers; they look like a rowing team.

An inebriated one at that.

I wait for the guys to resume their revelry before leaning toward Michael and whispering, "What did you say to them?"

"I told them you were my love slave."

"Ouch. A little too close to the truth, don't you think?"

"I'm kidding," he says. "I introduced you as my secretary. It is what you told the maître d', after all."

"Sorry about that. Not too believable, huh? I said 'assistant,' by the way."

"Better than claiming to be my niece, I suppose."

"Funny, the thought did cross my mind."

Michael shakes his head, amused. "Hey, kiddo, I'm forty-two, not sixty-two."

"Thank God for that," I say.

I watch him calmly take a sip of his red wine, his hand steady as a rock. Amazing. Not only doesn't he flinch when I unexpectedly appear at his business dinner, he invites me back and introduces me to his clients, all nine of them.

That's balls.

That's Michael.

"So, to what do I owe this unexpected pleasure, Madame Secretary?" he asks.

"I needed to see you," I say. I don't elaborate, of

course. I can't get into it right here. I wouldn't even know where to start.

"You know I was going to call you later, right?"

"Yes." I half smile. "I guess I couldn't wait." I pant a little against his ear.

"Ooh, I like the sound of that. *Check, please.*"

Before I can say anything more, Michael turns back to the table and shows off some more of his Swedish. Again, I have no idea what he's saying.

But when he finishes, everyone reaches for a pen.

Chapter 16

"WHAT DID YOU SAY to them *this* time?" I ask.

I'm following Michael out of the dining room. He answers over his shoulder, "I'll tell you in the limo."

We bolt from the restaurant and Michael takes my hand. Then he lets go right away—and starts to yell.

Not at me, though. He's screaming at a street person urinating against the side of the building. "You piece of shit, you moron, you walking obscenity!"

He pushes the man, and his face hits the brick wall. I look away. This is the thing about Michael that I don't like at all—his temper. It doesn't show itself often, but when it does, *look out*.

I walk on ahead and he catches up, takes my hand again. "Sorry, Kris, sorry," he whispers. "Sorry, sorry, sorry."

A little way down the street, his driver, Vincent, is already out of the company limousine and he opens the rear door for us. I didn't even notice he was parked there when I arrived.

"Here, Vin," says Michael, handing him a folded

hundred-dollar bill. "Can you buy me a pack of Luckies, please?" Michael doesn't smoke.

Vincent, a large man who looks as if he just walked off the set of *The Sopranos,* gives a quick and firm nod. Enough said. He closes the door behind us and promptly gets lost.

Michael and I settle into the plush leather backseat. He dims the lights so they're just right.

"Alone at last," he says, stroking my hair. "I'm *really* sorry about back there."

"It's okay. You're too protective, that's all." I give him a playful poke to the chest. "Okay, so now tell me: why did everyone at the table offer you a pen?"

"It's called, God is in the details."

"What's that supposed to mean?"

Michael unbuttons my jacket and begins to kiss my neck. He's a terrifically good kisser, and massager, and tickler.

"I told them my secretary had brought some contracts that I'd forgotten to sign earlier today back at the office."

He slides his hand underneath my sweater, unhooking my bra.

"Then, for good measure, I told them I didn't have a pen on me. Suddenly, they're all so busy looking for one that they never bother to wonder if I'm actually telling the truth."

He cups my left breast, caressing it slowly. He's a good breast cupper and caresser too. Michael definitely has the touch.

"That's what separates the good liars from the bad ones—going the extra mile, adding that little nuance. *Details,* my dear."

"You're crazy, you know that?" I say.

"Crazy for you, anyway."

Then Michael reaches down and begins to unbutton my jeans. I can feel myself getting wet and incredibly hot.

Wait. Stop. Hold it.

"Michael, there's something I have to tell you about—"

But I only get partway into the sentence before he covers my mouth with his. He kisses me deep and hard, and I get caught up even more in the moment. He feels so good, and I feel so safe in his arms. And, need I say, *sane.*

We fall back against the length of the seat, the leather cool and enticing to the touch. He pulls off my jeans, and I help him out of his trousers. His hand slowly travels up my thighs, over my stomach, around my chest, his fingers barely grazing my skin.

"God, you're amazing," he says. "So soft, so sweet. So *not* Penley."

I wrap my legs around Michael tightly as he enters me, and I don't let go of him until I come.

I feel dizzy and wonderful and I never want the feeling to end.

Not ever.

This is no dream.

Chapter 17

"SO, WHAT DID YOU WANT to tell me?" asks Michael, tucking in his shirt. "Did something happen today? Something good, I hope. That gallery called?"

But somehow I don't feel like a postsex conversation. Honestly, what happened today seems too crazy to talk about now. I feel embarrassed. I'm also whipped.

"We'll talk about it tomorrow," I say. "You've got to get back to your dinner."

He grasps my hand. "Are you sure?"

I nod. "Pens or no pens, your guests might be a little suspicious by now."

"That, or just more drunk."

I laugh and he smiles. *God, I'm still helpless in front of that smile of his.*

Michael pages Vincent to have him come back and drive me home. Putting down his BlackBerry, he begins to fidget with his tie.

"Here," I say. "Let me do that."

As I flip up his collar and straighten the knot—always a double Windsor—he gently caresses my cheek.

"I love you. I adore you. You know that, right?" he asks.

"Do I?"

"You better."

I give him "the Look," the same look I've been giving him for months now. He knows what's coming next and playfully rolls his eyes.

"Go ahead and say it, Kris."

You bet I will.

I lean over, whispering in his ear the two words that will make all the difference—the one thing he absolutely needs to do.

"Dump Penley."

For some added incentive, I gently lick his ear and blow. He recoils like a little boy being tickled. I kind of like that too, his vulnerability at times.

"I'm working on it," he assures me.

"Truly?"

"Truly." He reaches into his pocket. "And in the meantime, there's this."

He pulls out a narrow rectangular case—red leather with a white bow.

I can feel the smile breaking out on my face. "Oh, you're scoring some huge points tonight, Turnbull!"

"I do play to win, don't I?" He places it in my hand. "And no, it's not a pen."

It certainly isn't.

Slowly, I open the elegant case, the hinges providing just enough tantalizing resistance.

Then I stare in disbelief.

It's a bracelet. A diamond-and-sapphire bracelet! The sparkle is so bright my hands are glowing.

"It's so beautiful!" I gush.

"Just like you," says Michael. "Here, put it on. No, let me do it for you."

He gently snaps it around my wrist, and I can't take my eyes off it. Partly because I love it, but mostly because it's from him.

"So, do you like it?" he asks. Then his voice becomes low and soft. "I'm always afraid when I pick out things for you. I want you to be happy."

"I love it! I love *you!*"

"Good answer."

I kiss and hug him, squeezing tight. "Thank you, thank you, thank you!"

"Let me see that wink of yours," Michael says.

So of course I wink, my killer wink.

"Just promise me one thing," he says with a grin.

"What's that?"

"Don't wear it to work."

Chapter 18

I KEEP STARING AT my stunning, unbelievably beautiful bracelet as Vincent drives me home.

Four diamonds ... two sapphires ... four diamonds ... two sapphires ... all the way around my wrist. *A perfect circle.*

Well done, Michael!

It's almost enough to make me forget why I came rushing down to see him in the first place. Not quite, but almost. I'm certainly glad I did, though. Already, my awful day seems like a long time ago. That's a very good thing.

The limo eases to a stop at a red light, and Vincent asks me if the temperature is okay "back dere."

I glance up at the nape of his thick neck, where a jagged scar protrudes from beneath his shirt collar. "It's fine," I answer. "No, it's perfect. Thank you for asking, Vincent."

He's driven me home a handful of times, and we've yet to have what could be considered an actual conversation, though he's always very nice to me. It's funny how big guys like him are never much for small talk.

Then again, it could also be due to my feeling a bit awkward around him. I mean, he knows what's going on. In a way, he's a conspirator.

Michael says he trusts "the big guy" more than anyone, and by all indications, he has every reason to. Vincent has been his driver for over nine years. Not only does he predate me, he predates Penley.

Still, it makes me a little uncomfortable that he knows about us, that anybody does.

We ride the remaining blocks in silence, and my eyes take turns between the bracelet and the view out my window. The glistening lights, the people, the buildings—the city can be so hypnotic at night.

"Here we are, Ms. Burns."

As he always does, Vincent steps out and opens the door for me in front of my building. I take his arm at the biceps and he guides me to the curb.

"Thank you," I say.

"You're welcome."

Closing the door behind me, Vincent is about to climb back into the limo. I feel as if I need to say something, though I'm not sure what. Anything, I suppose, to ease the awkwardness. It's about time we said something beyond general niceties.

"Can I ask you a question, Vincent?"

He turns to me. "Yes, Ms. Burns?"

I sputter for a moment. Then some words come. "Do you like your job?"

"Yes, very much so," he says. "Mr. Turnbull is a good boss."

"I'm sure he is. I know he trusts you a great deal."

He nods.

"You're pretty loyal to him, aren't you?" I ask.

Vincent pauses for a second. He's probably not sure where this is going, and to be honest, neither am I.

"Extremely loyal," he answers.

"That's important."

"Yes, it is, Ms. Burns." He folds his arms. "There's nothing I wouldn't do for him."

"Good answer," I say.

Chapter 19

I JOLT UP FROM MY BED midscream, but I'm holding it inside because I don't want to explain myself to Mrs. Rosencrantz again. I'm soaking in sweat as tears race down my cheeks, the images still burning in my mind.

From the dream . . . which feels so incredibly real.

I've had it again, the exact same one. *I don't believe this!*

It's the next morning, but that's all that's changed. I even hear the music, that same song playing in my head. A familiar tune, though I still can't put a name to it.

And the smell of something burning is present too. Just like at the Fálcon. *What is that smell?*

Swinging both feet out of bed, I take a second to wipe my eyes dry. I feel miserable and drained. Not even the sight of my beautiful new bracelet curled up on the night-stand can raise my spirits.

It isn't as if I've never had a recurring dream before. I've had plenty — only they're the ones you read and hear about, the anxiety dreams apparently everyone shares, like being naked in public or showing up unprepared for the big college exam.

This one is different.

This dream seems to be all mine, nobody else's. The Fálcon Hotel. Why there of all places? Four dead people. Who were they and how did they die?

I check my alarm clock. Like yesterday, it's a few minutes before six. I can sleep a little more if I want to. *Yeah, right.* As if I really want to invite the dream to come back.

Dragging myself to the bathroom, I immediately make the mistake of looking in the mirror. *Ouch.* This could be worse than yesterday. Staring back at me could easily be the "before" picture of a face-lift.

Hey, at least I've got hot water today.

With the shower on full blast, I crank my Wet Tunes, the hope being that I can drown out one song in my head with another. Better yet, maybe they'll play the same song, so I can hear the lyrics and figure out what it is.

Somehow, I don't imagine myself being that lucky.

The shower does feel good, though, so I stay in there for a while. As the water cascades over my head, I begin to relax. I've got the radio tuned to WFUV, the college radio station out of Fordham, and they're playing "Alison" by Elvis Costello, one of my favorites.

Before I know it—and just as I hoped—it's the only thing I hear between my ears.

That is, until the song ends and some guy comes on reading the news.

I whip back my head from the shower spray. I could swear he said something about a tragedy at the Fálcon Hotel.

But that's not what has me shaking like a leaf as I try to towel myself dry.

The radio newsman didn't say it happened yesterday.

He said it happened *this morning.*

Thirty minutes later, Michael hasn't called, but I'm heading out the door of my place. I turn my key to double-lock it. *And*—

"Ms. Burns? Ms. Burns?"

Not again. It's way too early to face the Wicked Witch on Nine. I turn—and it's even worse than I thought. Mrs. Rosencrantz has brought a bald old man, who towers over her despite his being no more than five-foot-five, -six tops.

"You were screaming and screaming," she practically screams in my face. "You woke up my Herbert. He heard it. Ask him, Ms. Burns."

I don't ask Herbert. I scurry away. I don't even use the elevator; I take the stairs. *Hurry!*

Chapter 20

EVEN BY MANHATTAN STANDARDS, I'm walking incredibly fast a few minutes later. People are parting for me left and right. I'm a sidewalk Moses.

Next stop, the Fálcon Hotel. Probably the last place in the universe I want to visit. But I have to go there.

Sure, a cab would be quicker. But I'd prefer not to freak out while trapped in a moving vehicle.

No wonder I'm thinking again about my ex-shrink, Dr. Corey. While puffing away on his pretentious pipe, he would espouse these little self-help mantras. Things like "Hang tough!" and "Face your fear!" and "You have to take responsibility for your own life."

Back then I thought they were all pretty silly, clichés — not unlike a psychiatrist who smokes a pipe.

Yet here they are, sticking in my head, a blast from the past. And they actually seem to be working a little.

I pick up the pace. Only a few more blocks to go.

I can feel the undertow grabbing hold now, sucking me in. *Why am I so drawn to this hotel?* Well, I happen to know the answer to that one, but it's a secret I'm taking to my grave. *The secret of the Fálcon.*

Reaching to my side, I pat my shoulder bag for the outline of my camera. I know it's there; I checked as always before exiting my apartment, but I'm leaving nothing to chance.

The speed walking breaks into a jog as I cross over Park Avenue at 68th Street. Up ahead, around the corner on Madison, is the Fálcon.

My heart starts to pummel my chest, and I can feel the veins in my neck throbbing.

You can do this, Kris. Nobody is going to solve this but you.

I'm steps away from the corner. Do I hear a crowd still gathered? Is that a siren? There's only one way to find out.

But my feet have other ideas.

I stop shy of the corner, fighting the undertow and giving in to my fear. I'm afraid to look.

Don't be such a wimp!

That's not exactly one of Dr. Corey's mantras, but it does the trick just the same. Taking a deep breath and balling my fists, I push around the corner and stare.

At absolutely nothing.

What I see is a typical New York street scene outside the Fálcon—people coming and going, cars and cabs sputtering along in front of the hotel's bright red awning. It's as if nothing happened.

Duh. *What was I thinking?*

Obviously I misheard the guy on the radio. I was under the shower, after all. Too much water in the ears.

That has to be it.

I reach for my camera. These won't be my most inspired pictures, but they may be among my most satisfying. *See, Kris, you're not as crazy as you thought.*

And after clicking away, I'll go inside the hotel and ask the front desk what happened *yesterday*. I'll get the story, the scoop, the truth. Then I'll put this whole bizarre thing behind me.

I lift the camera to my eye, my hand reaching to focus. I'm twisting the lens clockwise when I feel someone touch my shoulder.

I freeze.

Like a picture.

Click!

Then—*crash!*

The camera slips from my grasp, falling to the pavement.

Chapter 21

DAMN IT TO HELL! I stoop to pick up the Leica. Still in one piece, but the lens shattered on impact.

Then I spin around—and it's his eyes I see first, the same intense stare as yesterday. It's that detective, the thin older man who smells of aftershave and tobacco and has that look that says "I know you did something."

He stands there, dressed in what appears to be the same dark gray suit, as I try to catch my breath. He says nothing—not even "Sorry I startled you." Instead, he seems to be suppressing a smile. *What, this is funny to you?*

Suddenly, I don't care how foolish I might look to him.

"Do you always sneak up and scare the hell out of people?" I ask him angrily. "You have some nerve."

"I was hardly sneaking," he says.

I watch as he pulls out a pack of Marlboros, shaking a cigarette loose. His hands are huge, knotted and gnarled. This guy works for a living.

"So, what brings you here?" he asks, lighting up, then inhaling deeply, enjoying it. "Or should I say, what brings you *back* here?"

It's a simple question, certainly not unexpected given the circumstances. Still, I immediately get this vibe from him. He isn't so much asking as he is interrogating.

"I'm on my way to work," I answer. "This is the route I take every day. Most days."

He exhales a thin stream of smoke from the corner of his mouth. "You want one?" he asks, extending the pack.

"No, thanks."

"You sure?"

"I don't smoke," I say.

"You used to, though."

"What makes you think that?"

"The way you're looking at the cigarette," he says. "Desire is an easy read with people—especially with the things we know we shouldn't do. I'm a *detective*. Homicide."

He's right. I used to smoke. More than a pack a day, in fact. I started after I moved to New York. Not that I'm about to admit it and give him the satisfaction.

He takes another long drag and continues to stare at me. "Of course, there are so many things that can kill you in this city, what's one more?"

It's the perfect opening to ask him what happened—who were the people in the hotel and how did they die? But again there's that vibe. Is he trying to get me to talk about it? If so, why? What could I know about four strangers?

"What brings *you* back here?" I ask instead.

And like that, he grins. Not unpleasantly, and he seems more human. "Sometimes the bad guy is dumb enough to return to the scene of the crime," he says. "Or bad *girl*, as the case may be."

So much for that vibe being just a vibe.

"What did you say your name was again?" he asks.

"I didn't."

He reaches into his jacket. Out come a ballpoint pen and a notepad. "Any time you're ready," he says, poised to write.

"Are you interrogating me?"

"No, I'm just asking for your name."

"It's Kristin Burns," I quickly answer. "And yours?"

He stares at me. *Those eyes.*

"Delmonico," he says. "Detective Frank Delmonico."

He reaches into his jacket again and hands me his card. I don't look at it. On purpose. Instead, I glance at my watch.

"Listen, I'm sorry to cut this short," I say, "but I'm afraid I'm going to be late for work."

It sounds like such a line, and for the most part it is. Then again, this guy has never encountered the wrath of Penley "the Pencil" Turnbull. As much as I want to hightail it out of there, I also need to. Otherwise, Detective Frank Delmonico might be investigating another death, this time up on Fifth Avenue. Mine.

"I promise," I say. "If we can do this later, I'll answer any question you have. But I don't know anything. Just tell me where we can meet."

He snaps his notepad shut. "Don't you worry your pretty little head," he says. "I'll find you. It won't be a problem."

Then he touches one finger to the side of his temple. "Detective, remember? Homicide."

Chapter 22

HUFF AND PUFF, huff and puff.

But Penley isn't waiting for me at the door when I arrive for work. I guess that's my reward for sprinting the last few blocks up Fifth Avenue so I wouldn't be late.

I've barely taken two steps into the apartment's foyer, however, before I hear her lovely voice call out from the kitchen. "Kristin, is that you? Tell me it's you."

"Good morning, Penley," I answer.

Though, like yesterday, it's been anything but a good morning. In fact, with the repeat of the bad dream, having to see that creepy detective again, and, in between, shattering one very expensive camera lens, the morning so far has been downright awful. One of my worst ever.

I walk through the red velvet–lined dining room with its crystal-dripping chandelier and push through the swinging door of the white-on-white-on-stainless kitchen to see Penley sitting over a cup of coffee.

Huh?

Sitting next to her is Michael.

Great . . . just great.

This is hardly the first time the three of us have been in the same room together, but it's the last thing I need right now. Of course, Michael's probably getting a big kick out of it.

Or maybe not.

Actually, he doesn't look too chipper as he glances up from his *Wall Street Journal*. With bleary eyes, rumpled ash-blond hair, and his body wrapped sloppily in a robe, hungover would be more like it.

"Be careful we don't talk too loud, Kristin," says Penley in a sarcastic whisper. "Someone here was out a little late with the boys last night."

"You're lucky it was the Swedes and not the Russians," says Michael, barely above a mumble. "Otherwise, I'd still be in bed."

"Oh, yes, how *lucky* for all of us," says Penley, rolling her eyes. She actually gives me a smile, as if the two of us are sharing some kind of female-bonding moment.

Pu-lease.

Michael's evening with the Swedes must have gone on long after he said good-night to me. Long, *long* after, I should think, as he's rarely late for the office.

The only other time I saw him like this was when Penley last took the kids out to her parents in Connecticut for the night and Michael stayed in the city, claiming he had to work. The two of us snuck off to Brooklyn, grabbed a back table at a restaurant, Bonita, and drank three pitchers of sangria. We woke up the next morning—in a suite Baer Stevens keeps on Central Park South—with headaches the size of Mexico.

Penley glares at Michael. "Well, aren't you at least going to say hello to Kristin?"

"Hello to Kristin," he parrots, his eyes not budging from the newspaper.

Penley whacks his arm, and I do everything not to smile. In his efforts to keep her in the dark about our relationship, Michael has mastered the art of complete indifference toward me when the three of us are together. So much so that it's comical.

Not to mention pretty smart.

Seconds later, Penley assures us that the ruse is still working. After informing me that Dakota and Sean are in their rooms, getting dressed for school, she turns to Michael as if she's just thought of something.

"Hey, what about Kristin?" she says. She turns back to me, not waiting for Michael to respond. "I mean, I've never heard you talk about having a boyfriend. I assume that means you're available. You are, right? Available?"

Available for what?

She explains, "I was telling Michael about this guy I know at my gym who was upset about his girlfriend leaving him. *I* think what he needs to do is start dating again as soon as possible. Would you like to meet him, Kristin? He's cute."

"You mean, like a blind date?" I ask.

"Call it whatever you want."

I glance at Michael, who raises an eyebrow. His "Ignore Kristin" facade looks to be crumbling at the prospect of my going out with another guy who is "cute." Nonetheless, there's not much he can do or say at that moment, and we both know it.

"Gee, Penley, I don't know," I hedge.

She shrugs. "What's there to know? Unless, of course, you're gay — which is nothing to be ashamed of, mind you. You're not a lesbian, are you, Kristin? You can tell me."

I shake my head, utterly speechless.

"Oh, *goody,* it's settled, then!" says Penley, over the moon. "His name is Stephen. I'll tell him all about you and we'll set something up. He is a hunk, Kristin."

Gee, I can't wait.

Chapter 23

PENLEY SURE KNOWS how to clear a room.

She saunters away to organize a guest list for her latest charity benefit. This one, gag me, is for the Elementary Etiquette Society and involves Dakota and Sean, poor kids. "Then it's off to the gym."

Michael leaves to take a shower and get changed—finally—for work.

And I go to grab the kids for breakfast.

"Good morning, princess," I say, peeking my head into Dakota's pink-and-lace room to see her sitting on the edge of her canopy bed, reading *The Trumpet of the Swan*.

She looks up and gives me one of her heart-melting smiles. "Good morning, Miss Kristin."

"All dressed?" I ask.

Dakota glances down, frowning at her Preston Academy uniform. It's an adorable green-and-blue plaid skirt with a simple white top, but for a young girl who has to wear it every day, it might as well be a burlap bag.

"Yes," she groans, "I'm dressed."

"Meet me in the kitchen, okay? I'm going to check on Sean."

She holds up the book. "I'll be there in one more page."

I continue down the hall, marveling at how much Dakota loves to read. So will Sean, I bet, as soon as he learns how, which we're working on. Besides being loved, is there anything better for a child? I doubt it.

Arriving at Sean's doorway, I see him sitting on the floor, immersed in a sea of Legos. Last month, all he built was rocket ships. This month, it's nothing but cars, albeit with "super-duper special powers."

"What does that one do?" I ask.

Sean turns to me, his small face beaming. "Hi, Miss Kristin!" He presents his latest contraption in the palm of his little hand. "This one shoots lasers and missiles and can bust through anything. It can also go under water."

"That's very cool, Sean." *You're very cool, m'boy.*

"Oh, and it also makes ice cream!"

Naturally.

I look him over, head to toe, making sure he's properly, or rather *prep*-erly, dressed. My eyes stop abruptly on his bare feet. *This* will not do at the Academy.

"Where are your socks, Sean?"

"I don't know. No idea. I want to wear my Jimmy Neutrons, but I can't find them."

"Maria might have left them in the laundry room. I'll go check, sweetheart."

I head for the very back of the apartment, past a huge storage closet, and flip on the light for the laundry room. Sure enough, I see Sean's Jimmy Neutron socks—named for the Nickelodeon cartoon character with the huge head and the pompadour—sitting on top of the dryer.

As I reach for them, I hear a mischievous whisper over my shoulder.

"Want to join the Maytag club?"

Chapter 24

I TURN AROUND to see Michael grinning from ear to ear. I shoot him a dubious look and whisper back, "Maytag club?"

"Yeah, it's like the mile-high club, only with a spin cycle."

"Very funny."

"I'm serious," he says. He's still in his robe, though it's now open down the front. "I want you right here."

That gets him the mother of all dubious looks from me. "Sure, and when Penley wanders in, I suppose you'll be able to explain everything."

He laughs. "This is the laundry room, Kris. It's the *last* place Penley would ever wander into."

He has a point there.

Still.

"Go and take your shower," I say, and push him away. "Better make it a cold one, buster. Thanks for thinking of me, though."

Instead of leaving, Michael takes me in his arms and

begins to gently kiss the curve of my neck. He knows I like this a lot. Usually.

I stand there, not giving in. "What happened to your hangover?" I ask.

"All of a sudden I feel a lot better."

I glance down. "I can tell."

He pulls me closer, his lips moving toward mine. Michael has beautiful, sensuous lips that are nearly impossible to resist.

But I'm still not giving in. "This is about Penley setting me up with that guy, isn't it? The *cute* guy. Stephen."

"Not at all." He leans back, gazing into my eyes. "You're not really going to go out with him, though, are you?"

"I knew it—you're jealous!"

"Okay, maybe a little. She is *such* a bitch. Phony, condescending, sadistic."

His hand glides down my stomach. He reaches into my pants, his fingers disappearing between my legs.

Damn. There's nothing more sexy to me than a very confident man displaying a dash of vulnerability.

I start to give in a little. We've never done anything like this in the apartment. Not even the couple of times we've been here alone.

"Michael," I say, returning his kisses. "The children."

"They're fine."

Not if they see this.

I know this is wrong, that I should stop. This is so bad. But it feels so good. And Penley *won't* come in here.

I undo Michael's robe all the way and stroke him with my hand. It's as if I've lit a fuse. He's very hard and very large.

Quickly, powerfully, he grabs my shoulders, spinning

me around—as promised. Down go my pants and my underwear.

I reach and grip the back of the washer, the metal cold against my bare thighs. He enters me amid a swell of goose bumps, and after only a few swift thrusts I feel myself ready to explode.

"Miss Kristin, where are you?"

Sean's little voice filters in from down the hallway. Michael and I both freeze in place.

"Did you find my Jimmy Neutron socks?" he calls out.

"Tell him you'll be right there," whispers Michael, slowly beginning to thrust again.

Feeling every inch of him inside me, I can barely speak. The moment couldn't be more dangerous.

Or more of a turn-on.

The socks are still in my hand, and I squeeze them tight as my body tenses, quivering.

"Miss Kristin?" Sean calls out again. "Are you there?"

Michael takes hold of my hips, thrusting faster and deeper, faster and deeper. My head whips back, my toes curl, and then my entire body completely lets go.

"I'm coming!"

Chapter 25

CONNIE SQUINTS AND MAKES a funny face, which is just what I need right now: *funny.* "They really should pass out flashlights with the menus, don't you think?"

"Either that or pay the electric bill," jokes Beth.

My two best New York friends and I share a knowing laugh, keenly aware that our restaurant of choice this evening—the very dimly lit and ultrahip Bond Street—is a far cry from our usual, more modest haunts. In the heart of downtown, the place offers Japanese cuisine at its trendiest and most expensive. The sake alone goes for twenty dollars a serving. Yikes!

I raise my palms. "Speaking of *paying the bill,* what on earth are we doing here?"

"You said you needed a night out, Kris, so I figured we'd splurge a little," says Connie. "You're worth it, sweetheart. Besides which, the Abbott Show is going to call any day now, any *second,* so we're pre-celebrating."

I glance down at the menu with its skyrocket prices before looking back up at Beth, the struggling actress, and Connie, the social worker with the city's Division of Family Services.

We're splurging, all right.

"So how's the Pencil?" Beth asks.

"Thin and mean as ever," I answer.

"Why doesn't she like you, Kristin? I don't get it. Who wouldn't like you?"

"Actually, I'm not sure Penley likes anyone. After two years, though, you'd think she'd at least trust me with the kids."

Connie chimes in with a smile. "She probably thinks you're writing the sequel to *The Nanny Diaries*."

We all laugh at that one.

"Seriously, if you hate this wretch of a woman so much, why do you keep working for her?" asks Beth. "This stepmom from hell."

"The kids," I reply. "I love them. And they really do need me."

Never mind their father.

There have been so many times I've wanted to tell Beth and Connie about my affair with Michael. Maybe I haven't because I'm embarrassed or ashamed—which I am. Or maybe because I know what they would say—"Be careful, Kristin; you could really get hurt"—and I don't want to hear it. Especially because they could be more right than I'm willing to admit.

So I keep Michael to myself. From time to time I tell the girls about having a few dates with some made-up guy. The script is always the same: he seems so promising at first and then turns out to be a loser of one kind or another. At no point do Beth and Connie question my continuing bad luck with men because such is life for a single girl in Manhattan.

Or is that true everywhere? It was definitely that way for me in Boston.

"What can I get you this evening?" asks our waiter, almost sneaking up on us. He's dressed in black, head to toe.

The three of us order a small feast, and when it arrives everything is delicious. At least, I'm pretty sure it is. With all the drinks we're also having, my taste buds are getting a little numb.

And I'm starting to get buzzed.

Soon there's no recurring dream, no weird pictures in my darkroom, and no guilt over Michael and me in the laundry room this morning.

"C'mon," says Connie, "the night is still young and so are we. This is Kristin's night!"

We head from the restaurant over to the Luna Lounge on Ludlow Street and check out a band called Johnny Cosine and the Tangents that Beth read about in the *Village Voice*. What a riot! Four guys who look as if they met in their high school math club. They wear nerdy clothes and pocket protectors, and play these great, silly songs like "Slide Rule Love" and "I Think You're Acute."

Connie, Beth, and I dance and laugh hysterically together, having an absolute blast. It's nights like this that remind me how truly wonderful this city is and that, damn it, I am young and I have great friends!

"Don't look now," says Beth with an elbow to my ribs, "but I think that guy's checking you out."

Chapter 26

I TURN AND SEE HIM immediately. He's sitting at the bar, staring directly at me.

Instinctively, I look away. I don't think it's anything about him, just the circumstances of the past couple of days.

"See what I mean?" says Beth with a playful smile. She spins around, her arms swaying to the music. "I'll leave you two alone! He's cute, Kristin. Remember, this is your night."

I turn back to the guy, and our eyes lock. He's nicely toned, with a chiseled face and long blond hair tied in a ponytail. He could be European—French, perhaps. Then again, he could be from SoHo. Or Portland, Oregon. It's hard to tell these days.

Either way, I don't think he's my type, whatever that is.

But the eye flirting is kind of fun. It's not like I'm cheating.

I wait for him to do something—a smile, a nod, a wave, anything.

Nothing.

He just continues to stare in my direction. He barely even blinks. What's his deal?

The dance floor goes dark. The band starts up with another song—something fast, disco-like—as a beam of light hits a mirror ball hanging from the ceiling. The room begins to spin.

Through the dizzying lights, I glance at the guy with the ponytail again. He's still looking at me.

Ignore him.

I turn my back and move closer to Connie and Beth, forming a triangle. We get tighter and tighter as more people spill onto the dance floor. It's really packed. I can feel the floorboards shaking beneath my feet.

Is he still staring?

Don't look.

But I want to know. I *am* buzzed, after all.

I lean in, shouting over the music to get Connie and Beth to check for me. "At the bar . . . the one with the ponytail," I say.

"Where?" asks Connie, her neck craning.

"I don't see him anymore," says Beth.

I turn and he's gone. All that remains is an empty bar stool.

Okay. That's fine.

"Let's dance," I say to the girls. "It's my night."

Chapter 27

MAYBE TWENTY SECONDS LATER, the guy with the ponytail is walking toward Beth, Connie, and me, slowly weaving his way through the traffic jam of people on the dance floor. He's wearing a black suit and white shirt, open collar.

My instinct is to give him a wink—just a little one. But I don't do it.

"Beth? Connie?" I say.

They can't hear me. They're so wrapped up in the music, they don't even notice I've stopped dancing.

He's getting closer, and maybe because of what's happened lately, my skin is starting to crawl.

"Beth! Connie!" I say again.

But the music's too loud.

A strobe light kicks in, hurting my eyes. It's like a million flashbulbs going off, one after the other. I can't see him anymore, and that makes it worse because I know he's there. And getting closer.

There he is!

A dozen feet away.

What does he want?

He's stopped in the middle of the dance floor. It seems as if everybody in the club is moving except for the two of us.

His blank stare is gone. In its place, a slight smile. I get the feeling he knows me, or at least knows who I am. This isn't a chance encounter, is it? Could he be a detective? Maybe he works with the older, skinny guy? That makes some sense to me, as much as anything does lately.

He comes up to me and stands maybe, *oh, I don't know,* two feet away.

"You were watching me," I say. "You were staring."

"You caught me. You're very pretty, y'know. You must know that?"

I do—kind of. Usually I dress down, but not tonight. Maybe because I feel safe with my girls around.

I start to say something, but he raises his hand and cuts me off. Like he's used to being in control.

"Listen. You seem like a nice person. You ought to really watch yourself. Be careful, huh?" He leans in real close. Too close. "I'm not kidding around. You've been warned."

Chapter 28

NOT AGAIN.

Please, not again.

I awake the next morning to everything repeating itself. Well, actually, that's not accurate.

This time I open my eyes to total darkness. Not the darkness of a room in the middle of the night. Like—nothingness. Blackness.

With a sound track—that unidentified song playing in my head.

Then comes *picture*—the dream—the four gurneys, the hand emerging from that body bag . . . and I'm jolting up in bed, screaming, sweating, trembling.

I hear a loud banging, only it's not at my door.

This time it's coming from my ceiling, or rather, from the apartment above me. Apparently it's not only Mrs. and Mr. Herbert Rosencrantz I'm waking up at the crack of dawn.

"Sorry!" I shout out. I truly am.

Double sorry because it's Saturday.

I hope my upstairs neighbor will be able to get back

to sleep. As for me, I know I can't. Or won't. As exhausted as I am from being out last night with Connie and Beth, I'm not about to close my eyes again. It doesn't matter that I've got the weekend off. My dream—this nightmare—doesn't.

Besides, how could I sleep with this music in my head?

It's still there—the mystery song. Worse, I think it's getting louder.

Or is that just my head throbbing? Yesterday was Michael's turn to have the hangover; today it's mine.

Slowly, I will myself out of bed and into the bathroom, where I shake a couple of aspirin into my hand, washing them down with some New York tap.

Then it's straight to the kitchen to make some coffee.

I'm not much of a java junkie and usually only drink the stuff for "medicinal purposes." *Like now.* A while back, though, Michael turned me on to Kona coffee from Hawaii, and I've been loving it. I get it over at Oren's Daily Roast on 58th Street.

Michael's particular about his coffee but not really in a snobbish way. The only reason he doesn't like Starbucks, he says, is due to the "laptop losers" who treat the place like their own personal office and hog all the seating. One morning I saw him go a little nuclear on a guy who was using two chairs for just his knapsack.

Sipping a cup of Kona in my kitchen, I try to get a handle on the growing weirdness of the past few days. Is that even the right word for it, I wonder? *Weirdness?*

Maybe there's more to this than I realize. Or maybe it's the opposite, and I'm overreacting.

Or maybe I'm simply thinking about it too much. It's not as if I have a solution to make it stop.

I'm weighing that last possibility when the phone rings.

It's awfully early for someone to be calling. The caller ID says "Operator." Strange.

I pick up. "Hello?"

The operator sounds close to being a recording without actually being one. "I have a collect call from Kristin Burns. Will you accept the charges?"

Clearly the coffee hasn't kicked in yet because I could've sworn she said a collect call *from* Kristin Burns.

"I'm sorry, *who's* calling?"

"This is the operator."

That part I got.

"No, I mean, who's trying to call me?" I ask.

"Hold on a second, please." There's a click on the line, and she's gone for a few seconds before returning. "It's Kristin Burns," she says.

Is this some type of joke?

"Michael, is that you?" I ask.

There's another click, and I wait.

But the operator doesn't come back.

No one does.

The line goes dead.

I guess Kristin Burns doesn't want to talk to me after all.

Chapter 29

I'M NOT SURE WHAT to think after that phone call except that I *really* don't feel like hanging around my apartment. Maybe because I'm shaking and I can't make it stop.

As for the word *weirdness* to describe what's going on, it's officially far too mild a term.

At times like this, *as if there's ever been a time like this before in my life,* I try to think of a bigger picture. For example. One second the whole universe was smaller than the head of a pin. The next second it was billions of times larger than the Earth. And the lesson to be learned from the big picture is exactly *what?*

Thankfully, there's an errand I have to run. Errands are good when you think you might be going stark-raving mad. So after showering and getting dressed, I hail a cab for Gotham Photo over in Chelsea. I've got a camera that needs a new lens.

"Hi. Is Javier here today?" I ask, walking up to the counter at Gotham. I notice that my shaking has finally stopped. Hey, the song in my head is gone too.

"He's in the back," says the clerk. "Is there something I can help you with?"

"If you don't mind, I'd like to wait for him."

"Sure, I'll let him know," he says. "You're Kristin, right?"

"Yep. Hi."

The entire staff at Gotham Photo is friendly and they all know their stuff, but Javier's my favorite. He's always able to explain some of the more technical aspects of lenses and film without making me feel like an amateur. Truly, he's as nice as can be.

"How are you, Kristin? It's good to see you," he greets me, smiling. He's tall and thin and cultured, with a very gentle way about him.

We chat for a bit about anything and everything — so long as it has to do with photography. This isn't merely a job for Javier; it's more like a calling. He loves cameras that much. "My mother bought me my first, a Rollei Thirty-five when I was six years old," he once told me.

I believe it.

"So when am I going to read about you in *Blind Spot*?" he asks. That's the hip magazine that covers the famous as well as up-and-coming photographers.

"Just as soon as I get a new lens," I answer.

I tell him about breaking mine, and we get busy choosing a replacement. After discussing a few, we settle on the latest Leica, which he highly recommends.

"It's lighter and shoots cleaner," he says. "And the best part is that I can give it to you for over a hundred dollars less than the one you had."

Twist my arm, Javier.

As he writes up the sales slip, I casually tell him about

the transparent-like effect happening with the pictures I developed from the hotel. Unfortunately, I didn't think to bring the shots with me. I do my best to describe the glitch, but without Javier's being able to see it, he can offer only educated guesses. Most I've thought of, a few I haven't.

"Of course, if it had anything to do with your old lens," he says with a grin, "your problem is solved."

I'm anxious to find out, so I start taking pics the moment I leave the store. I want a full roll to develop when I get home later.

After snapping a few shots of a meticulously groomed Lhasa apso being walked by a woman who looks like Nancy Reagan, I head north and come upon two block-shaped movers struggling to load a huge armoire onto their truck. Both their faces twist and contort so horribly that it's absolutely beautiful.

Click, click, click.

I smile to myself. I never feel more comfortable, more at home, than I do behind a camera. It's so relaxing and yet, at the same time, so empowering. You see people in an entirely different light. Sure, they say the eyes are the windows to the soul, but for my money it's the camera eye that gives you the real glimpse of what's inside a person.

I've got a few more shots left on the roll as I'm aiming at the stream of people crossing the street up at the next "Walk" sign. They move in almost perfect unison and yet remain oblivious to one another, all looking directly ahead at the coming sidewalk.

All, that is, except for one.

It's a man standing still at the corner. He's caught my eye.

I focus on his face, watching in the viewfinder as the image slowly transforms from blurry to —

Holy shit!

Staring back at me, clear as day, is something I can't believe. Not even after what's happened during the last few days.

Something impossible.

Something that makes me feel that I *must* be crazy.

Only it's worse than that, because I know I'm *not* crazy.

But what I'm looking at sure is.

Chapter 30

I'M SHIVERING UNCONTROLLABLY and that burning smell is in the air again, but my lens remains focused straight ahead. *On him.*

He's standing on the far corner, wearing a long single-button gray coat that looks as if it came from one of those vintage clothing stores over on Bleecker Street.

Only I know it didn't come from some shop on Bleecker or anywhere else in New York. Actually, it's from Concord, Massachusetts.

Suspicious, I lower my camera as if somehow this piece of metal and molded plastic in my hands is the culprit, the cause of all this.

It's not.

I can see clearly with my own eyes. The square jaw, the bullet-shaped head, the thick glasses, even the narrow, hunched shoulders. It's him.

My father is standing there on that street corner.

Don't think, just shoot.

Quickly, I snap a few shots, even though my hands are jiggling the camera insanely. Then I call out.

My father sees me, I *know* he sees me, but he doesn't answer.

I take a few steps forward and call out again, louder. "Dad!"

He's looking right at me. *Why won't he say anything? Or wave? Or something?*

I continue toward him, and at last he reacts.

By walking away! Fast walking. As if he's afraid of me or something.

"Wait!" I yell. "Dad! Please don't go. I need to talk to you!"

He disappears around the corner, and I immediately sprint after him. Crossing the street, I see him farther up the block. He's running now.

What's going on? What can this possibly mean?

I call out again, begging him to stop. "I just want to talk to you! Dad! Dad! Daaad!"

We were always so close, practically inseparable. When I was a little girl, he used to pretend to race me all the time. Back then I knew he was letting me win because he loved me so much.

He wasn't letting me win now, though. Obviously not now.

Chapter 31

I'M RUNNING AS FAST as I can. The sidewalk is crowded, and I try my best to weave in and out of pissed off–looking people while keeping an eye on the gray coat and crew cut head bobbing farther up the block.

"Hey, watch it!" a woman barks angrily, as we slam shoulders.

"Sorry," I say.

My father turns another corner. Then he darts across an intersection, just as the light turns green. Cars, cabs, and trucks hit the gas.

But I don't stop. I don't even look both ways. I have to catch him—nothing is more important. I'm convinced he's the answer to everything that's happening.

Leaping from the curb, I hear tires screeching and feel the hot breezes kicked up from the asphalt by one near collision after another. The huge chrome grille of a bus misses me by less than a foot. "What the hell is your problem, lady?" yells the driver out his window.

You have no idea.

"Please, Dad! Please stop!" I yell. *"Daddy—please!"*

And just like that, the gray coat comes to a halt. My father turns on the sidewalk, and our eyes meet. We're maybe fifty feet apart.

"I want to help you," he says. "But you have to do it yourself."

"Dad, what's happening to me?"

"Be careful, Kristin."

I open my mouth to ask, Why? How? What is it that I have to do? but he takes off again before the words can form.

I cave in to my emotions, collapsing to the pavement. My palms are skinned raw as they break the fall. I look up helplessly and catch a final glimpse of his head disappearing around the next corner.

Meanwhile, people form a circle around me, watching and wondering what my problem is. I know that look. I've *given* that look.

They think I'm crazy.

"You don't understand!" I tell them, tell anyone who'll listen or even stare down at me with a look of disdain. "You don't understand!"

My father's been dead for twelve years.

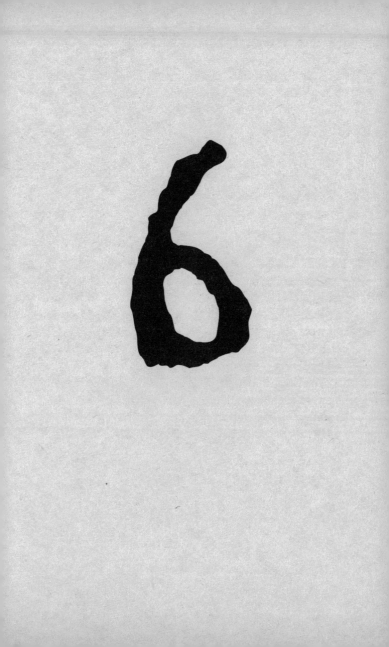

Chapter 32

ANYWAY, AFTER SEEING my dead father, I can't get home fast enough, though it's the very place I had to escape from less than an hour ago.

In the cab back to my building, all I do is stare at my camera and wonder about the film inside. I squeezed off three, maybe four shots of my father. I can't remember exactly.

But all I need is one.

What's scarier—that it's really him or that it's all in my head?

Practically busting through the front door to my apartment, I make a beeline for the darkroom. And hopefully some answers.

"Hurry up!" I implore the film as it stews in the processing tank. "Move it!" I think this is the only time I wish I owned one of those instant cameras.

I'm so single-minded about getting these shots developed that for a few minutes I don't pay the slightest attention to what's all around me. Pinned to the corkboard walls are the pictures from the Fálcon, a morbid exhibit if there ever was one.

But once I notice them, I can't keep from looking at them.

Bad idea.

Also, on one corkboard are some old shots from my days growing up in Concord, Massachusetts. My mother, my father, my two sisters. And one shot of my boyfriend from college, Matthew, with his head cropped off—which is so richly deserved.

"Hurry up!" I yell again at the developing film.

Finally, there's something to see.

I pull up one of the shots, staring hard at the image. The gray coat, the hunched-over posture—the man whose casket I saw lowered into the ground back home with my own eyes. *It's my father.*

My eyes tear up as I grab another shot and then another, poring over every detail.

Suddenly, it's as if I'm chasing him all over again. I'm out of breath, my chest burning. The room feels as though it's caving in, and I reach out for the wall to steady myself. *So this is what a panic attack feels like. . . .*

Desperate for air, I flee the darkroom, and when that's not enough, I run around opening all the windows in my apartment.

I try to breathe normally, but I can't.

C'mon, Kristin, keep it together. Somehow, some way, this has to start making sense. You just have to find the organizing principle.

It *wasn't* my father, I tell myself, just someone who looks like him. Maybe someone's trying to mess with my mind. It's got to be something like that.

Christ, how insanely paranoid can I get? Someone messing with my mind? Who?

Out of nowhere, a sharp pain shoots straight up from my feet. My thighs and calves are throbbing, and I can't stand it anymore. Not any of this.

Balling my hands into fists, I begin to pound at my legs. I'm literally beating myself up.

"Stop it! Stop it! Stop it!"

Closing my eyes, I let go with a primal scream, and yet at the same time I have a very sane thought. *This is no time to be alone.*

Chapter 33

I CALL MICHAEL.

Actually, I page him. That's how we work it on the weekends. The *arrangement* between us.

I'm the supposed big client to whom he gives direct access 24/7, so Penley doesn't raise a tweezed eyebrow when he disappears into his study to call me back on his private line. I even have a name. Carter Whitmore. Sort of sounds like a guy in finance.

Two minutes later, my phone rings. I don't bother with hello and cut right to the chase. "I need to see you."

Before Michael can respond, I realize how that sounds, or at least how he might interpret it. *Sexually*.

"I mean, I need to talk to you," I tack on. Strangely, I'm feeling better now. Calmer.

"Okay, so let's talk."

"Where can I meet you?"

"Oh," he says haltingly. "We can't do this on the phone?"

"I'd rather not." *Tell you that either I'm cracking up or it's a whole lot worse than that.*

"You sound stressed. Is everything okay?"

"No," I answer. "Can't we meet somewhere?"

"That's the problem. I'm about to take Dakota and Sean to the Central Park Zoo."

"Perfect. I'll meet you there. Ten minutes."

Silence.

"What is it, Michael?"

"The kids," he says.

"What, don't you think they'd like to see me?"

"Of course I do. That's my point, Kristin. They'll like it so much it will be the first thing they tell their mother when they get home."

"Then what if I just happen to bump into you guys?"

He chuckles in a way I immediately don't like. Almost condescending. He can be that way, but not with me.

"I think you're reaching," he says.

Now I'm a little pissed. And yes, I am stressed, okay?

"You're right, Michael, I am reaching. I'm reaching out to you now, and you're not there for me."

"C'mon, don't be so melodramatic, Kris. Take it all down a notch."

I press him. "What about later? Are you free after the zoo?"

The silence again says it all. "I can't," he responds. "I would if I possibly could. Penley made plans tonight with another couple."

I'm about to vent the mother lode of frustration and a whole lot worse on him when he abruptly clears his throat.

"I'll check on those figures for you, Carter. I'm on it," he says in his best business voice.

Shit.

"Penley just walked in, didn't she?" I say.

"Yes, Carter, that's correct. You have such a good feel for these things."

I listen to Michael babble on about debt ratios and the nonfarm payroll report. *Give him credit, the switch over was seamless.*

"Okay, she's gone," he says seconds later.

"What did she want?"

"The kids are waiting on me, so she was pointing at her watch and making an incredibly bitchy face—then again, what else is new?"

I can't help a slight smile. I am calmer now, and I love it when he dumps on Penley. All the better for my Dump Penley campaign.

"So where were we?" he asks.

"Your not being there for me," I answer.

Michael sighs. "I'm so sorry, honey," he says. "Tell you what. How's this? We're supposed to drive out to Connecticut tomorrow to see my in-laws. I'll do like I did last time and tell Penley that something came up with work. Better yet, I'll blame it on you, *Carter.*"

"Can you really do that? "

"Sure. We can spend the whole day together, maybe drive upstate and have a picnic somewhere, and you can tell me whatever it is you want to talk about."

The thing is, I want to tell him now—*right now*. At least I think I do. Which raises an interesting question. How much do I really trust him? This much?

"Michael, I—"

"Oh, shit," he interrupts, sounding rushed. "Penley's heading back this way. I'll call you tomorrow morning, okay?"

There's no time to respond.

He's gone.

I hang up as if in slow-motion. It's hard to put the feeling into words. Empty? Numb?

Still alone?

Usually, just the thought of being with Michael makes everything better. No longer. At least not today. Because tomorrow isn't soon enough for me.

Right away, I pick up the phone again.

There's somebody else I need to call.

Actually, this should have been my first call.

Chapter 34

"THANK YOU FOR SEEING me on such short notice, Dr. Corey."

I watch as my ex-therapist slowly — and I mean *slowly* — fills his pipe with tobacco from a plastic bag. I swear, glaciers move faster.

But it's okay. I'm going to get some help.

"To be honest, Kristin," he says, his eyes fixed on his pipe, "I'm not particularly happy about this appointment. However, given the way you sounded on the phone, the sheer desperation in your voice, I felt a professional obligation to see you. So here we are. What can I do for you?"

Gee, Doc, that really makes me feel welcome.

Still, it's okay. I'm lucky he was able to make time for me.

A few Manhattan psychiatrists keep weekend hours, and Dr. Michael Roy Corey is one of them — at least during the spring, summer, and fall. That's when he works Saturdays so he can take Mondays off to play golf at some public course near his house in Briarcliff Manor.

"No crowds on the course and my pick of tee times,"

he once explained to me. That was about a year and a half ago, when he first became my therapist. Six months later, I stopped seeing him. I thought I'd worked out my issues.

Not that I could see these new ones coming.

I lean back into his familiar gray leather couch and describe some of the events of the past few days, culminating with spotting my dead father this morning. Dr. Corey listens while puffing away, not saying a word.

When I finish, I stare at him with expectant, hopeful eyes. *Let the healing begin!*

"Are you absolutely sure that's your father in the photographs?" he asks, tugging at a fold in a salt-and-pepper sweater vest that almost perfectly matches his hair.

"As sure as I can be," I reply.

"What's that supposed to mean, Kristin?"

There's a slight edge in his voice. Impatience, perhaps? Skepticism?

"It means I'm almost positive it was him."

"*Almost* positive, as in, it could've been someone who looked a lot like him."

"I considered that. But he spoke to me. And then why did he run?"

"Any number of reasons," he answers. "Maybe the man you saw didn't want to be photographed. I don't know; maybe he's wanted by the police. Maybe he's impaired."

I shake my head. "No, he even had on the same coat Dad used to wear. I'm *sure* it was him. I told you—he talked to me. He knew my name."

"So what you're saying is that your father, who's been dead for twelve years, simply *shows up* one day on a Manhattan sidewalk and starts up a conversation?"

"Yes, I know, it sounds nuts. God, do I know. That's why I'm here."

"Oh, I see, *that's* why you're here," he says, that slight edge in his voice getting sharper, louder. "You want me to *help* you."

What's going on here? This isn't what I need now.

"Yes, of course I want you to help me. I'm feeling pretty desperate, actually." My voice starts to crack on that last part, and I command myself to hold it together, if only for the sake of my dignity.

Dr. Corey removes his pipe and glares at me. "Listen to me, Kristin. For the last time, you need to get this through your head. Your father committed suicide and nothing you do or say is going to bring him back."

"I know that."

"Do you?" he asks, folding his arms. "Perhaps if you had continued with your therapy, this wouldn't be happening."

"But it's not just my father. What about the recurring dream?"

"We all have recurring dreams."

"This one came *true*."

"That's what you tell me. Of course, that doesn't make it so, does it? Listen to yourself. Are you listening to yourself, Kristin?"

I stare at Dr. Corey in, well, disbelief. This isn't the same guy who cheerily used to offer up those self-help mantras. He's Dr. Downer now. Or maybe it's only me he's down on. *Is he pissed that I stopped seeing him?*

"Don't you understand what I'm saying, Dr. Corey? All these strange and bizarre things are happening to me. They're really happening. I'm starting to think that I'm going insane."

"Maybe you are. Who am I to say?" he replies matter-of-factly. "All I know is that I'm not about to invest my valuable time again in someone who treats therapy like a fad."

I knew it!

"I told you, I thought I was better," I explain.

He sniffs. "Yeah, you're *obviously* a lot better."

I'm in shock. He's so mocking, so disdainful. How can he act this way toward me? I was his patient.

"I don't have to sit here for this," I say.

"You're right. You don't. Feel free to leave at any time. Just like you did before."

My eyes start to well up. I can't help it. The shakes are back, and I'm trying to control them. I don't want his pity.

"Oh, spare me the waterworks, will you?" he groans. "And don't try that insipid wink of yours either."

"What's *happened* to you, Dr. Corey?"

"Nothing. Nothing at all."

"It's clearly something, because you're being an incredible jerk."

"Better than an ungrateful bitch, I imagine."

That does it!

I spring from the couch and race out of there, but not without a parting shot from the door.

"Fuck you!" I scream.

"Go to hell!" he screams back.

And then, just as I'm shutting the door to his office, "I still want to know what happened to you at the Fálcon Hotel. Kristin? Kristin?"

Chapter 35

IT KEEPS GETTING WORSE.

The dream is even more vivid this morning. Actually, it's excruciating.

I wake up and smell that same burning smell. It's awful; I can't stand it.

The hives are back too. They're worse than ever, all over my hands, my arms, my face. I strip off my T-shirt, and there are red blotches on my chest and stomach, my legs, everywhere. I want to scratch my skin off.

And the music—that damn music—it's back inside my head.

The only saving grace? It's Sunday—I'm supposed to spend the day with Michael.

The phone rings at a few minutes after eight. The caller ID tells me it's him. *I bet he uses the line about the phone sex wake-up call.*

"Hello?"

"Hi," says Michael.

It's only one little word, one meager syllable, and yet

I realize right away from how he says it. Something's wrong. *Something else.*

"I'm not going to like this, am I?"

"It's fucking Penley," he says. "When I told her about not going to her parents', she went ballistic. She's still in orbit. Sean is calling her Penley Neutron. You know, like—"

"Yeah, I know, the cartoon." And his favorite socks, remember?

I feel like a fool standing in little else besides my socks, scratching red patches all over my body.

"You explained it was a work emergency, right, Michael?"

"Yes. But she didn't want to hear it, especially since that was the reason I didn't make the trip to Connecticut last time."

"She really cares that much if you go?"

"Christ, I don't know. She kept saying how much I'd be disappointing her parents."

"That's it, isn't it? This is about her *father.*"

"You don't have to say it like that."

"Why do you kowtow to him so much?"

"It's not so simple, Kristin."

No, it isn't. There's a certain undercurrent to Michael and Penley's marriage, all but unspoken. Michael makes a lot of money. In the millions. But it's chicken feed compared with the fortune that Penley's father, Conrad Bishop, sits on. The man was CEO of Trans-American Steel for twenty-five years. He's worth north of $200 million. More to the point, thanks to his country club buddies, he's thrown a lot of business Michael's way. I mean, *a lot* of business.

"If anyone, Penley's father would understand your having to work," I say.

"Maybe the last time I canceled," Michael replies. "Twice in a row, though, and it looks like I'm shunning him. It's disrespectful."

"So what are you telling me?"

He takes a deep breath and exhales. "That I'm going to Connecticut today."

The words sting like a million bees.

"But I really need to see you," I plead.

"I know, I know. I'll make it up to you, I promise."

The anger, the disappointment, the *hurt*—are too much for me, and I slam down the phone. It's the first time I've ever hung up on Michael, and I feel absolutely terrible.

Like I could die.

And then I notice something—the hives, the burning odor, and the music are gone.

What's up with that?

Chapter 36

THE ELEVATOR RIDE DOWN to the lobby feels as though it takes an eternity. I'm doing everything I can to keep my emotions in check.

I plead with myself, *Think calm thoughts! Think good thoughts if that's possible.*

Dispensing with visions of babbling brooks and sleeping babies, I go straight to what always works. One after the other, I conjure up my favorite photographs.

The nudes of Edward Weston.

Avedon's portrait of Truman Capote flashing his belly button.

And, of course, Annie Leibovitz's incredible shot of Yoko Ono and a naked John Lennon cuddling.

It's always about people with me, flesh and bone. I can appreciate Galen Rowell and Ansel Adams, but mountains and other landscapes never pack the same punch for me as a living, breathing person.

The mental slide show works, and I begin to settle down. That is, until I step off the elevator and spot my neighbor Mrs. Rosencrantz. Standing by her mailbox in an orange-and-blue circa 1973 muumuu, she looks up from a catalogue and shoots this incredibly evil sneer my way. *What is her problem?*

Clearly it's me.

I try to ignore her as I head for the door, but I can feel her eyes boring into me from behind those cheap large-rimmed glasses she wears. Her stare is relentless, she won't give it a rest; and as much as I want to keep walking out to the street, I can't help making a little detour. Right up into her face.

Whipping out my camera, I aim the lens an inch away from her pointy nose.

"Take a picture, you old bag, it lasts longer!" I yell.

Click.

I spin around, not waiting for her angry reaction. Everyone else in the lobby is now staring at me, but I say nothing more. I aim for the exit and look straight ahead.

What's come over you, Kristin?

This is so unlike me. I simply don't do things like this, yelling at people, getting in their faces.

It's scary.

And yet, scarier still is that I *enjoyed* it.

With everything happening lately, I'm acting more and more on impulse—thinking, saying, and doing things I normally don't. Those little red flags, the ones that are supposed to pop up in my brain, have mysteriously disappeared.

"Hey, watch where you're going, lady!"

It takes me a second to realize that the grunge-looking guy playing guitar for tips on the corner is talking to me. I nearly plowed right into him.

"Sorry," I mutter.

I'm already a block from my building, head down and

oblivious to everything and everyone. The guy's right; I need to watch where I'm going. Of course, that raises a good question. Where *am* I going? I stand still for a moment, thinking of what might have been. My day with Michael, the picnic he mentioned. We'd talk, hold each other, drink some wine . . . and I'd feel so much better.

Instead, I feel as if my day is ruined before it even started. The dream, the burning smell, the rash . . .

Then, out of nowhere, I have an idea.

Something a little, well, crazy.

Very unlike me. At least the way I was until a few days ago.

"Hey, lady, you mind moving along? You're hurting business."

I turn to the stringy-haired guy plucking away on his guitar, every other chord off-key. His ragged guitar case lies open at his feet, and I glance at the torn black velvet lining sprinkled with spare change. And I do mean spare. A quarter or two is the mother lode for this troubadour.

"I'm serious, lady," he barks. "Beat it! Get out of here!"

Before I know it, I'm right in his face too. "Listen, you sorry-assed Kurt Cobain wannabe, did you ever think that maybe it's your *playing* that's hurting business and not me?"

He's speechless, songless too, and I'm already halfway down the block.

I've got somewhere to go after all.

Chapter 37

WHEN I LEFT BOSTON and traded the Red Sox for the Yankees, I brought three things with me to Manhattan. A suitcase. A boyfriend.

And Bob.

There are undoubtedly far more inspired nicknames for a pickup truck than Bob, but I've always liked the simplicity of it. Besides, we're talking about a 1980 Ford F-100 with more than 180,000 miles on it. Even the rust has rust. A fancy name just wouldn't feel right.

I hurry over to First Avenue, where I park Bob at an outdoor lot. The indoor garages can cost more than some apartments here—like mine, for instance. Still, I don't get off cheap. Three hundred and fifty bucks a month, to be exact. That makes broken-down Bob, with his missing hubcaps and leaky engine, my greatest luxury in this city. Crazy, huh?

But today he's worth every single penny. Today Bob screams freedom, maybe even salvation.

The crosstown traffic is its usual bear, and I'm worrying that I might be late. When a Macy's delivery truck ahead of me doesn't move the nanosecond a light turns green, I obnoxiously bang on my horn. It doesn't take much to bring out my inner cabdriver.

Approaching the building, I know I can't park too close. Bob doesn't exactly blend in.

After circling the block a couple of times, I luck out with a spot that's a safe distance from the entrance. I reach for my cell and dial the apartment, hitting *67 first to block the caller ID.

Michael answers.

Good, they haven't left yet.

For the second time this morning, I hang up on him. Then I adjust my sunglasses, sink down in Bob's front seat, and get busy.

Waiting.

Soon I see Michael emerge from the building. I immediately want to rush out and go to him, kick his shins, and call him a nasty name. Then I'll kiss him so hard he can barely breathe. We'll escape to the nearest alley and have amazing, passionate makeup sex — no, wait, better yet, we'll *fuck,* like rabbits, like minks, or like whatever other furry creatures top the most-horny list.

"Have a nice day with your in-laws!" I'll say when we're done.

Instead, I stay right here with Bob, watching.

Michael disappears around the corner. A few minutes later, he returns with the "family car," a shiny black Mercedes, the G-class.

Almost on cue, Penley, Dakota, and Sean come bounding out to the sidewalk while Louis, sweating in his doorman uniform, brings up the rear with the kids' knapsacks and an overstuffed beach bag.

Michael steps out and straps Sean into his booster seat while Dakota climbs in on her own. Penley meanwhile opens a compact and applies some lipstick, blindly gesturing to Louis to load everything in the back of the wagon.

It should be me getting in that car, not Penley. That's all I can think as I stare at them. I should be the fourth in that particular foursome.

They may look like the picture-perfect family — all smiles as they pull away from the curb, heading for "the country" — but I know better.

Pictures lie.

Chapter 38

MICHAEL DRIVES LIKE a speed demon, hardly a surprise. It dawns on me that I've never seen him behind the wheel of a car before. I drove him somewhere once in Bob. Other than that, we're always either in his limo or taking cabs.

He's definitely a little reckless today, especially with the kids in the car. A couple of times I almost lose them, first by the George Washington Bridge and then later on I-95 through Stamford, where one of the lanes is closed for construction.

I tailgate other cars, trying to stay hidden in Michael's rearview mirror. For my first time following someone, I think I'm doing a pretty good job.

Next exit, Westport.

It's only an hour's drive from the city, but it might as well be a million miles away. So many trees, so much space, it's a whole other world. A very rich one, at that.

And the closer we get to the water, the richer it gets.

The homes looking out on Long Island Sound all seem to share this majestic, otherworldly quality. Beyond their manicured front lawns and perfectly aligned shutters, there's a certain grandness to them that goes beyond size. It's not mere money, it's wealth.

Michael turns into a driveway.

Fittingly, it belongs to the most impressive home of them all, a cedar shake Nantucket colonial that looks like a page out of *Architectural Digest*. Actually, make that *two* pages. The huge house rolls across the property like a wave, seemingly endless.

So this is where Penley grew up.

I park by the far end of the house behind a low hedge. I'm mostly shielded while still having a decent view of the grounds, including the large infinity pool and the tennis court. What I expect to see, I don't know.

What I'm even doing here is a much better question. We'll find out, won't we?

I watch as Michael and the rest of the Turnbull family spill out of their Mercedes wagon.

An older couple—Penley's mother and father, for sure—are quick to greet them with hugs and kisses, the majority going to Dakota and Sean. Penley's father kind of reminds me of a retired Gordon Gekko.

Sitting inside Bob and taking it all in, I imagine the conversation. Does Michael begin his ass-kissing right away with the old man or does he wait a bit?

They all disappear inside, though not for long. Dakota and Sean come racing out the French doors on the side of the house, heading straight for the pool. A woman wearing a uniform that screams "maid" isn't far behind. It seems that she's on lifeguard duty. She's sort of the day-in-the-country *me*.

Meanwhile, Michael, Penley, and her parents settle

into the whiter-than-white wicker furniture on the porch.
Yet another maid appears with a silver tray. The Norman
Rockwell image is slightly blown by the martini pitcher
taking the place of lemonade.

Fiendish ideas dance in my head. What if I were to
make a grand entrance? The emerging bitch in me imag-
ines what a scene that would be. "What are you doing
here?" Penley would ask, as I walk up to the porch.

"Why don't you ask Michael," I'd answer calmly.

Go on, wiggle your way out of this one, stud.

But I remain with Bob and instead reach for my camera. I snap shots of the kids splashing around in the pool.
It was only last summer that Sean still needed his floaties.
Dakota, on the other hand, is very graceful in the water,
a baby swan.

Out of nowhere, Penley marches into frame. She
barks at the kids, probably something about eating lunch,
because when she turns to leave, Dakota and Sean reluctantly climb out of the pool and towel off. They are adorable! And Penley is just awful.

As the kids amble back toward the house with the
maid in tow, my attention wanders. I'm gazing around,
admiring the neighborhood. Everything is so clean, the
air blowing in from the water so crisp. A few cars drive
by, all but one a convertible. And why not? All this fresh
country air to suck in.

I watch a woman in Nike everything jog by. Then
I spot a man in the distance, walking toward me. He's
wearing a light Windbreaker and a gray baseball cap,
his pace nice and slow. No hurry—like everything else
around here.

I'm about to look away when my eyes stop.

There's something strange about him.
Familiar.
My God, it's that detective from the Fálcon.
Frank Delmonico's here in Connecticut.
That just isn't possible, *but there he is.*

Chapter 39

I QUICKLY DUCK BELOW the steering wheel. The detective said he'd find me again. He warned me. *But out here?*

How did he know? Did he tail me as I followed Michael out of New York? I guess that's possible, but I sure can't have him asking more questions. Not right in front of Penley's parents' house.

I hear his footsteps now, louder and louder. They sound heavy, deliberate. He's a man with a mission, isn't he? But I don't know anything about those four murders. Why would he think otherwise?

Slowly, I peek over the sun-bleached vinyl of the dash.

The ball cap is pulled down over his eyes. Maybe it's *not* Delmonico. Whoever it is—I should get out of here right now.

I reach for the keys, snapping my wrist hard to the right. The ignition sounds with a lazy sputter, the engine cranking and cranking. *No!* It won't turn over.

C'mon, old buddy, don't fail me now! This is important. If Penley sees me—

I floor the gas pedal, my foot thumping down hard.

Don't flood it, Kris. Bob, help me out here. Bob, ole buddy?

I spot the little chrome knob by the window on the passenger side. The lock. It's up. The door's unlocked!

His footsteps are close.

I lunge, my fingertips only inches away from the knob. *But it's too late!*

I hear him gripping the handle outside. The raw squeak of ancient metal hinges drowns out my scream.

He's opening the door!

Chapter 40

"WHAT THE HELL are you doing here? Are you crazy?"

I snap my head up, looking directly into his eyes.

Not Frank Delmonico's . . . Michael's.

I've never been so relieved to see somebody in my whole life. If only the same were true for him. He's obviously pissed. He's livid, actually. I've never seen Michael like this. He looks as though he might have a stroke, at forty-two.

I don't say anything. I can't. I'm still trying to catch my breath, figure out some insane excuse for why I'm here.

He stands in the open door, shaking his head. "Christ, did you *follow* us out here?"

But for me there's a much more pressing question. "Is he gone?" I ask when I'm able to speak.

"Is *who* gone? What the hell are you talking about? There is no one here but you."

I sit up, peering around like a periscope. There is no one else, not another soul out on the street. *No Frank Delmonico.*

I fall silent, feeling so stupid. And crazy. I don't know where to start with Michael. The dream? The scene at the hotel? Delmonico? The man with the ponytail? How can I make sense to Michael when none of it makes sense to me?

Michael's face is still beet red. "Why are you here?" he asks again. "Answer me, Kristin."

I stare blankly at him as he folds his arms. *Why am I here?* It's the question I've been asking myself all along.

"I . . . uh . . . I don't know," I say. "I mean, it's complicated, Michael."

"What kind of an answer is that?"

I open my mouth, but nothing comes out this time.

"Never mind," he says, nervously glancing over his shoulder at the corner of the porch where Penley and her parents are sipping martinis. "The important thing now is that you get out of here. Fast. This was a big mistake, Kris. Huge."

I tend to agree.

One more thing before I go. "How did you know I was here?" I ask.

"Even through bushes, Bob's pretty hard to miss. We're damn lucky I'm the only one who saw you."

And right then we hear —

"Miss Kristin!"

My eyes go wide, almost as wide as Michael's. Dakota's sweet voice is a dagger through both our hearts.

I force a smile, and for the first time ever with this little girl, it isn't genuine. "Hi, honey," I say.

Michael turns around. Dakota's standing by the hedge, wrapped in a red-and-white-striped towel, her blond ringlet curls wet from the pool.

"What are you doing here, Miss Kristin?" she asks.

It's officially the sixty-four-thousand-dollar question, and I still don't have an acceptable answer. Not for her father, not for her.

Michael looks back at me. I know we're thinking the exact same thing.

Just how mature for her age is she?

Does she suspect something? Does she even know what it *is* to suspect?

"Honey, come here," says Michael.

Dakota shuffles over to him, and he gently puts his arm around her.

"Can you keep a secret?" he whispers.

Chapter 41

I'M IN NO CONDITION to drive back to Manhattan or anywhere else. My eyes should be focused on the road, but all I can see is Dakota's innocent face as she listens to her father. *Can she really keep a secret?*

We can only hope.

Either way, I've got to give Michael some credit. Telling Dakota I was there planning a surprise party for Penley at "Nana and Papa's" country club was a masterstroke of quick thinking. His voice was totally calm, not a hint of panic. "It's really, really important that you don't say anything to Mommy so we don't ruin the surprise. Okay, sweetheart?"

Wow. Never has so much faith been put in the nodding head of a little girl.

And it's making me incredibly uneasy. Mostly because I hate lying to Dakota and getting her into the middle of this mess. She's just a little kid.

With Connecticut at my back, I approach the city and somehow navigate the ever-narrow FDR Drive on the East Side without causing a fifty-car pileup. Once I return

Bob to the lot on First Avenue, it's almost as if I can't remember being behind the wheel.

Now what?

It may be a beautiful day, but I don't feel like being outside anymore. Nor do I want to go back to my apartment. So I hop a cab downtown to the Angelika Film Center, where there's a director's cut playing of *Flirting with Disaster*. How appropriate.

All I want is light and funny, and thanks to Ben Stiller, I get it. In fact, as advertised in the lobby poster, I get an additional "six never-before-seen minutes" of it. I'm curious, though. Has a "director's cut" ever been shorter than the original?

After the movie I try to do some clothes shopping in SoHo, where most of my favorite stores are. But as I flip through the racks at Jenne Maag, Kirna Zabête, and French Corner—where I once saw Gwen Stefani trying on a pair of jeans—I'm just not in the mood. I keep regretting my very stupid trip out to Westport.

Even if Dakota hadn't spotted us, I really goofed. Michael had every right to be angry. Well, maybe not *that* angry?

What was I thinking?

For about the tenth time, I reach for my cell phone to call him. I want to apologize again.

And for about the tenth time, I put the phone away without dialing. *Don't push it,* I warn myself. I know how he is. If I let him be for a day or two, he'll be fine.

We'll be fine.

Chapter 42

WITH THE AFTERNOON sun waning, I stop on the corner of Prince Street and Greene, waiting for the "Walk" sign. I gaze around. A little paranoid. Not too bad, though. It's all relative.

If there's a better place to people watch than the heart of SoHo, I'd sure like to know about it. Maybe Paris? Maybe not. Society types, punkers, artists, a few cross-dressers, you name it, they're all out here sharing the sidewalk.

Including the nutcase on the corner directly across the street from me.

He's an old man wearing sunglasses and a long gray beard practically down to his belt. He's pacing back and forth, carrying a sign like in the classic cartoons. Only instead of "The End Is Near," his reads, "The End Is Just the Beginning." His take on the Resurrection, I guess.

Yeah, I get it—*I've been warned.*

As I cross the street and pass him, I can't help shaking my head. How does a person become so disconnected from the rest of the world?

"Be afraid, Kristin."

Huh?

I stop dead in my tracks, turning back toward the man. "How do you know my name?"

"I just know it."

I take a few steps closer. I'm about a foot from his face. He's definitely there. He's real. "I said, *How do you know my name?*"

"It's not too late, Kristin," he says. His voice is raspy, raw, a little scary on its own.

He tries to turn away, and I grab his shoulder. "Wait. What are you talking about?"

Silence from him now. *What—have I offended Mr. ZZ Top?*

"Tell me!" I insist.

He smiles, flashing a mouth of the most rotted, brown teeth I've ever seen. But I don't back away.

"Do I know you?" I ask.

Reaching up, he removes his sunglasses, and I gasp. Now I back up a step. One of his eyes is missing. There's nothing there but a dark hole that seems to disappear into his head. Is that possible? I almost expect worms or slimy white maggots to crawl out.

"Not yet," he answers. "But soon you will. When you figure out your life."

He puts his shades back on, nods, and then turns away.

Chapter 43

I'M TREMBLING AS the bearded, one-eyed joker walks off down the street. It's officially a toss-up now. *Where is it more surreal? Inside my apartment or out here?*

Hailing a cab, I decide being in my apartment might not be so bad anymore. Perhaps a nice, quiet evening at home will help calm the nerves. Then maybe I can figure this out, though I seriously doubt it.

In fifteen minutes, I'm there.

I begin with a superhot bath, the kind you need to ease your body into an inch at a time. I even add some herbal salts that Connie gave me for my birthday last year. "Soothing Citrus," says the label.

After lingering in the tub until I'm "Wrinkled Prune," I towel off, climb into my comfy terry cloth robe, and force myself to dial up some Chinese — sesame chicken and vegetable fried rice, my standard order. No MSG, please. I am trying my very best to have a normal night at home, which is ridiculous, I know, but it's the only idea I have at the moment.

On a full stomach, after the day I've had, I should be dead tired. Instead, I'm wide-awake. Restless. Wired.

I try not to think of the one-eyed man on the corner—*How did he know my name?*—but if it's not his face I'm seeing in my mind, it's another's. Dakota's.

"Miss Kristin?"

Her sweet voice echoing in my ears, I remember that I've got an entire roll of her and Sean in my camera, the two of them swimming and playing by the pool.

At last, something that might put me at ease.

My darkroom.

I literally roll up the sleeves of my robe and get busy. Almost immediately, I can feel my mind and body relaxing. I even crack a smile as I think of a great name for an exhibit. "Stakeout." It would be strictly pictures I've taken while parked somewhere, hiding.

No, wait, I've got an even better name. "Bob and Me."

This is more like it. Moving the negatives to the holding bath, I catch a glimpse of the first few shots from the roll.

"Oh, how cute!"

I actually say the words out loud. My two favorite kids in the world, splashing around and having so much fun. Even in the negative I can see their beautiful smiles.

It's a little weird, though. I always make a point of showing Dakota and Sean every picture I take of them. But these they'll never see.

Eventually, I get to the shot I snapped with Penley in it. So typical, her pointing and barking orders at the kids. She looks more like a warden than a mom.

I'm about to shift to the next picture when something

makes me do a double take, and my stomach just about drops to the basement of the building. I grab the magnifying loupe, pulling the image of Penley right up to my face.

I stare in amazement.

Utter. Freakin'. Amazement.

Chapter 44

I QUICKLY CHECK the previous shots, the ones of only Dakota and Sean. Is it happening with them too?

No. No, it isn't.

Everything looks fine. Better than fine, in fact.

I grab the shot of Penley again, staring, squinting hard, running my finger over it. The negative seems fine to me.

Her image, though. *Not fine. Not good. Not possible.*

It's that same effect as with the body bags outside the Fálcon, subtle yet definitely there. Or, should I say, not there.

Transparent. Like I can see through her. Like she's there but isn't.

Penley's thin, but she's not *that* thin! How is this happening again? Why?

I flip on the light, spinning around to face the black corkboard behind me. The other shots, my father—I never checked to see if the effect was happening with the photos of him. Did I just not notice?

My eyes race along every picture pinned to the wall,

and not a single one has the effect. *No problem with these shots—just a man who's been dead for twelve years!*

So it isn't the lens after all. The new one did the same thing the old one did. Must be the camera, then. At least I hope it's the camera.

I remember a business card that Javier at Gotham Photo once gave me. On the back he wrote his cell phone number. I think maybe he was fishing for a date. Nonetheless, he said I should call him anytime I have a problem with my pictures.

I think this qualifies.

The only question now is where I put that card. I start with my wallet, shuffling through ATM receipts, my AmEx, Visa, Discover, driver's license, a frequent-coffee-drinker card from the Java Joint.

Javier's card isn't there.

I check all the drawers in my bedroom, including the one in my nightstand. It's amazing how much junk I accumulate. Do I really have to take a book of matches from every restaurant I eat in, for God's sake?

C'mon, Javier's card, where are you?

I try to think back to when he handed it to me. When was it, what time of year?

Winter, I decide.

Maybe it's still in a coat. In fact, I'm pretty sure I know which one. A shearling I splurged on—a beautiful "just gotta have it" that I saw in the window at Saks. I ate a lot of tuna fish sandwiches for dinner that month, as I recall.

I also recall Javier complimenting me on it . . . *when he handed me his card.*

I'm pretty impressed with my memory as I head for the hall closet. Maybe I'm not *completely* losing it.

With any luck, I'll reach Javier and we can meet. I'll show him the pictures, he'll study my camera, and he'll tell me what's wrong. Simple as that. Mystery solved.

First things first, though—that card of his.

I open the closet door.

At least I try to. It's stuck. The knob twists, but the door itself seems to be jammed. *Oh, brother.* Now I'm not so sure I want to get into this closet.

But I have to, so I pull harder. Then harder still, with both hands. It's almost as if the damn door is locked from the inside; only that's impossible, isn't it? This closet's never been locked. Who would lock it?

Changing my grip on the knob, I really put some muscle into it. I yank so hard my shoulders ache.

Slowly, the door begins to give—until it flies open.

I look inside.

Oh, no! Oh, God! Help me!

And then I'm screaming at the top of my lungs.

Chapter 45

"KRISTIN, WAKE UP. Wake up!"

My eyes snap open, and I gaze around, confused and out of sorts. Not to mention petrified. Everything is soft focus. "Where am I?"

"You're in my apartment," says Connie. "On the planet Earth." She looks concerned, scared, even.

"Are you okay?" I ask her.

"Am I okay?" Connie shakes her head in disbelief. "My God, the way you were screaming, I thought somebody was trying to kill you in here!"

I can see sunlight slicing through the blinds. It's morning, and I'm lying on the pullout couch in Connie's living room on the Upper East Side, that much I've got figured out. Everything else is sketchy at best.

"I . . . don't . . . remember. . . ."

"You came here last night, *hysterical,*" explains Connie. "You were going on and on about this dream and some pictures you'd taken — oh, and you were telling me about your closet. The one in the front hallway? Is any of this ringing a bell?"

"The cockroaches . . ."

"Yeah, you said there were a million of them. It was horrifying just to listen to you describe it."

That's the last thing I remember. The entire closet was crawling with cockroaches. Maybe not a million, but a thousand, and I'm deathly afraid of cockroaches. They got in my hair, on my face. The rest is a blank.

Connie takes my hand. "You were quite the mess, sweetie," she says. "I gave you two Xanax and put you to bed. You slept straight through the night, not a peep."

Until now.

The hotel, the four gurneys, the hand. The same dream, only I had it in a different location. *It travels.*

"What can I get you, Kristin? How do you feel?" Connie asks.

Like shit.

With a sound track to boot. *Will I ever figure out what this song in my head is?* I wish Connie could hear it; maybe she'd know what it is.

But she can't. So I don't mention it, or anything else. If I don't understand what's happening to me, how could she? Plus, I don't want to frighten her any more than I have already.

I'm fine, I tell her. "In fact, what time is it?" I ask — panicked. "I can't be late for work."

I pull back the covers, and Connie stops me.

"Hold on," she says. "This is serious, Kris. You should've heard yourself last night, the things you were saying. Something's very wrong. I think you need to see that psychiatrist of yours again."

Been there, done that.

"I'm so sorry I scared you," I say. "I've been having

this recurring dream, and it seems so real. I guess I've been under a lot of stress lately."

"What about these pictures you were ranting about? Ghostly images? Transparencies?"

"Part of the dream," I lie.

Am I embarrassed about going bonkers? Ashamed? Why can't I talk to one of my best friends about this?

Connie regards me for a moment. "At least call in sick," she says. "You need to relax."

"I can't, Connie. The kids depend on me."

"Let the Pencil take care of them today. She is their *mother,* after all."

"Really, I'm fine." I fake a smile and swing my feet to the floor. Then I give Connie a little wink. "Do you think I can borrow some clothes?"

Chapter 46

DONNING A PAIR of black slacks and a putty gray turtleneck from Connie's closet, I'm out of her apartment in less than ten minutes. Normally it takes me a little longer to get ready for work. Then again, normally I don't have someone—in this case Connie—eyeing me as if any moment I might climb onto a chair and begin shouting, *"I'm cuckoo for Cocoa Puffs!"*

So as I walk into the Turnbulls' building and ride the elevator up to the penthouse, I experience something new and different. Being early.

Good. No chance of Penley waiting for me at the door.

Instead, it's Sean I see immediately. He's sitting on the floor of the foyer, engrossed in the bright-colored Legos scattered around him. He doesn't even hear me come in.

"Good morning, sweetheart."

Sean glances up, beaming. "Hi, Miss Kristin!"

I kneel next to him. "Whatcha building? Looks impressive. Sha-zam! What *is* that?"

"A supergalactic missile launcher that will save the world from the evil aliens of planet Thunder."

"Wow, are they planning to attack us?"

"I think so," he says with the cutest nod.

I automatically give him the once-over, checking to see that he's properly dressed for school. He is, from his head right down to his little toes, which happen to be covered by his Jimmy — or is it Penley? — Neutron socks.

"Where's Dakota?" I ask.

"She's in her room."

I straighten up, barely taking a step before Sean adds, "We're not supposed to bother her."

"What do you mean?"

"She isn't going to school today," he says, his eyes glued back on the Legos.

"Is she not feeling well?"

"I don't know for sure. Mommy seems pretty mad, though."

The words twist my stomach into a million knots. Maybe Dakota came down with a cold. *Or maybe she couldn't keep a secret.*

I kneel next to Sean again. "What did you hear Mommy say, sweetheart?"

He snaps another Lego into place. "Hey, look at this, Miss Kristin!" Sean makes a *whoosh!* sound, waving his missile launcher back and forth.

"That's neat," I say, struggling to be patient. "But can you tell me what Mommy said? You remember, Sean?"

My mind explodes with the thought of Dakota spilling the beans to Penley: "I saw Miss Kristin at Nana and Papa's house — she and Daddy were together!"

Is this how it ends? How this insane house of cards comes crashing down?

I peer over my shoulder at the door to the apartment.

The instinct rising inside me is like a power surge to the brain.

Run!

Get out of here!

You don't want to face her!

But before I can make a mad dash, I hear Penley's mincing footsteps around the corner of the foyer. I turn to look, and there she is, staring right at me.

"Speak of the devil," she says.

Chapter 47

"SEAN, DEAR, CAN YOU GO to your room, please?" asks Penley, her voice actually kind of gentle and sweet. *Too* sweet, I'm thinking. She's overcompensating for what's to come, the bloody showdown when it's just the two of us out here.

Is it too late to make a run for it?

Sean scoops up his missile launcher and shuffles off toward his room. I'm half tempted to beg him to stay. Penley wouldn't try to kill me in front of her stepson, would she?

Not knowing what to do, I stoop and begin gathering the remaining Legos on the floor.

"That can wait," she says. "Come, we need to talk."

Dressed in her workout clothes —*what else?*—Penley leads me into the living room, motioning for me to have a seat on the green satin couch against the wall. She takes one of the two armchairs facing it, and we both settle in.

"So, how was your weekend?" she asks.

I can't believe it. *She's toying with me!* The pleasant smile and friendly tone. She never asks about my weekend. Never.

"It was fine," I answer.

"Do anything special?"

"No, not really." *Oh, yeah, I did see and talk to my dead father. Almost forgot.*

Is she trying to get me to confess; is that her game?

Nothing doing. I'll tell her the same thing Michael told Dakota. We're planning her surprise party. *That's our story and we're sticking to it!*

"How about yourself?" I ask, matching her broad smile tooth for tooth. "Did you have a nice weekend?"

"Very nice," she says. "We spent yesterday out in the country at my parents' place."

"Oh?"

"I mentioned we were doing that, didn't I?"

"You might have." *Actually, you didn't, Michael did.*

"You know, you should come out with us sometime," she says. "It's on the water; there's a pool and tennis court. It's a very nice escape from the city."

Oh, you're good, Penley.

If this is how you want to play it, I'll make it easy for you. "Gee, I bet the kids really enjoy it."

"They truly do. What kid doesn't enjoy being around the water?" She folds her legs. "Strange, though."

"What's that?"

"Dakota."

Finally . . . here we go.

"Yes," I say. "Sean mentioned she wasn't feeling well."

"Actually, I'm not sure what's wrong with her. By the time we were heading home yesterday, she seemed a little off. She doesn't have a temperature, and it's not her stomach. Something's bothering her, though. Any ideas?"

I don't say anything. Every muscle tenses, and I brace

myself for the moment. Surely this is when she lays down her cards.

Instead, all Penley does is shrug.

"I'm sure Dakota will be fine. She's tough, takes after Michael," she says. "Just in case, I thought we'd keep her home from school today." She flicks her wrist. "Anyway, that's not what I wanted to talk to you about."

I barely manage a swallow. "No?"

"Guess who I spoke to last night?"

As long as it's anyone but Dakota, I couldn't care less at this point. I'm swimming in relief. "Who?" I ask.

"My friend Stephen."

It takes me a moment to connect the dots. "Oh, the guy from your gym—the cute one?"

"Exactly," she says. "The *very* cute one. So, tell me, do you have any plans for tonight?"

"Uh . . ."

"Because you do now."

Chapter 48

"DID YOU KNOW that some female cockroaches mate once and are pregnant for the rest of their lives?"

"Wow," I say, nodding my head and feigning amazement rather than repulsion.

The guy wipes his nose on his sleeve while making some weird clicking noise in his throat that I've never heard any other human make. "No wonder there are so many of the little suckers, right?"

"Yeah," I say. "No wonder."

Of course, things could be a lot worse. This guy could be my blind date for the evening. Instead, he's my nooner. The exterminator. On my lunch break, I meet him at my apartment. Actually, *outside* my apartment. There was no way I was going back in there by myself.

Anyway, he's a fittingly creepy-looking man with thick black-rimmed glasses that magnify his eyes. He sort of reminds me of Stephen King, the pictures I've seen of him, anyway. Of course, *pictures lie.*

"Thing is, cockroaches are basically built to survive

almost anything," he says. "Did you know they can hold their breath for up to forty minutes?"

"Interesting. You are full of information, aren't you?"

He adjusts his spray nozzle. "So, you saw them in the closet here, huh?"

I nod. *Yeah, just a couple thousand of them.*

"Then that's where we'll start."

"Sounds like a plan."

As he reaches for the closet door I stand back. I don't want to look. I don't even want to be here.

"Hmm," he mutters, looking around. "Mmm-hmm, hmm, hmm."

"What?"

"There's not a single dropping on the floor." As if correcting himself, he raises a palm. "Not that I don't believe you, of course."

I watch as he flicks on his flashlight, shining it against the closet walls.

"What about your neighbors?" he asks.

"What about them?"

"You all get along?" He wipes his nose on his sleeve again. "I've had situations where one neighbor sabotages another with cockroaches — you know, letting them loose in vents or through holes they drill. Happens more than you'd think."

I immediately try to picture Mrs. Rosencrantz, or her Herbert, doing something so wicked. I suppose I wouldn't put it past them.

We walk the rest of the apartment. Every nook and cranny gets sprayed and resprayed. A few times I even try to tell him that he missed a spot.

"What's in here?" he asks at the last door down the hallway.

"That's just my darkroom." I open the door for him, flipping on the light.

He walks in and looks around, intrigued. "Mmm-hmm, mmm-hmm."

After a few quick squirts of his spray nozzle, he notices the pictures pinned to the walls. He stops at one of my father.

"You know this man, don't you?" he asks.

"Why do you say that?"

"His expression—the way he's looking at you and not the camera. In fact, I'd say you know him quite well."

"You're right. He's my father."

He leans in, really examining the picture. "Was he a good man?"

"Excuse me?"

"I said, was he —"

"No, I heard you okay. That's kind of an odd question, don't you think?"

"Actually, I think it's the only question . . . for all of us, that is. In the end, we're only the sum of the choices we make, right?"

Oh, great, the existential exterminator.

I'm beginning to get the heebie-jeebies from this guy. It's bad enough that he looks creepy; does he have to talk creepy as well? I can feel an attack of the hives coming on.

"And how did you know my father is dead? You said, *Was* he a good man?"

He shrugs. "I guess I just assumed."

From looking at a recently developed picture of him?

We're talking serious heebie-jeebies now. This guy can't leave my apartment fast enough. It's possible that he's as scary as thousands of cockroaches all by himself.

"So are we all done here?" I ask hastily.

"I'm sorry. I've offended you, haven't I?"

"No, it's okay. I think I'm a little on edge thanks to the roaches." *Among other things.*

He pats his trusty spray canister. "Hopefully we've taken care of that for a while."

"About how long does the poison last?"

"A month or so."

"That's all? You'd think there'd be something better in this day and age."

"You mean something that lasts forever?"

"Exactly."

He shakes his head. "No, I'm afraid there's only one thing in this world that lasts forever."

"Let me guess. Love?"

"No," he says, leaning in close. "That'd be your soul."

Chapter 49

AT HALF PAST EIGHT, I walk into the bustling Elio's on Second Avenue near 84th Street and scan the bar area, keeping in mind the description I've been given. *Tall, dark, very handsome, answers to Stephen.*

If you say so, Penley.

You're the boss. And believe you me, if you weren't, there's no way I'd be going through with this blind date! Not right now especially.

"Excuse me, are you Kristin?"

I turn around and look up at a pair of amazingly high cheekbones. As for the rest of him, I take a quick glance.

Tall, dark, very handsome. *Check, check, check.*

"You must be Stephen," I say, and can't keep a slight smile off my face.

A minute later we're sitting at a cozy table for two along the wall. Michael would be *sooo* jealous.

But that's not why I'm feeling guilty. As Stephen and I talk and get acquainted—he owns a film editing company, likes to rock climb—it seems as if he's a genuinely nice guy. I feel bad that I'm wasting his time. My heart belongs to Michael.

After a few minutes, I think Stephen picks up on it. "Are you seeing someone?" he asks.

I feel even worse having to lie. "No," I answer. "There's no one."

"Penley told me you weren't, but I guess I wanted to make sure." He smiles. Nice smile too. "I should talk, right? I assume you heard about my situation?"

I shake my head. "Just that you recently came out of a relationship."

"That's one way to put it, I guess. Personally, I prefer the word *dumped*."

"What happened, if you don't mind me asking?"

"I made a mistake," he says, shaking his head. "I got involved with someone who's married."

Oh.

Thankfully, the awkward silence is broken by the waiter arriving to announce the night's specials. By the time he's done telling us about the veal osso buco, the blackened sea bass, and a "delightful" seafood risotto, I'm thinking it's safe to change the subject with Stephen.

Think again.

"So tell me more about your film editing company," I say as the waiter strolls off.

It's as if he doesn't even hear me.

"You know what the worst part is? I *believed* her," he says. "She kept telling me how she was going to leave her husband. I really should've known better. They never leave."

I immediately reach for my glass of water. My mouth is dry. Like I've been eating Saltines on the Sahara.

"Hey, are you okay?" he asks. "You look uncomfortable."

"I'm fine."

He sighs. "Jeez, listen to me going on and on about my ex. I apologize."

"It's okay. I understand."

"Do you?"

"Sure," I say. "It's not easy letting go." *I did it once, big-time. With Matthew of Boston.*

"You're right. But there's something else and it's been killing me."

"What's that?"

"The guilt. It never occurred to me until the relationship ended," he says. "I mean, where did I get off trying to break up a marriage?"

I hear him say the words and I have to remind myself that he's not talking about me. This is about *him*. But weirdly, I can't help feeling defensive. The parallel to Michael and me is unmistakable, and more than a little unnerving.

"Clearly this woman you were seeing doesn't have a good marriage," I point out.

"Yes, but good or bad it's still a marriage—I shouldn't have been trying to ruin it. They've got kids, for Christ's sake."

"But she doesn't really love them!" I blurt out.

He looks at me sideways. "Excuse me?"

Uh-oh. *Say something, Kristin. Anything! At least get your size eight out of your mouth.*

I clear my throat, trying to reel myself in. Then I put my hand on top of his. "I just think you're being too hard on yourself, Stephen. Remember, it takes two to tango."

"Yeah," he says, leaning in closer. "Except you're forgetting one thing."

"What's that?"

"No one's ever forced to dance, are they?"

Chapter 50

I NEED SOME AIR!

That's all I'm thinking as I say good-bye to Stephen. Our evening ends on the sidewalk outside Elio's with an exchange of awkward smiles, a peck on my cheek, and the unspoken understanding that this is our first *and last* date.

"Can I hail you a cab?" he asks.

"That's okay. I think I'm going to walk for a bit."

It doesn't matter where, and for the next hour or so, I pay no attention to the street signs. I wander aimlessly. It's only when I get a strange feeling in my stomach that I look up for the first time and see where I am.

Sixty-eighth and Madison, right smack in front of the Fálcon Hotel.

Coincidence?

I wish.

I'm starting to believe that everything is happening *for a reason.* If only I could figure out what it is. Something has to tie all this together, make sense of it.

Maybe the strangest thing of all: the Fálcon and I have

a history. Something I never talk about, not even to Michael. It happened my first week in New York, actually, just before I left Matthew of Boston. Since then, I try not to think about it. *But here I am!*

Standing in front of the hotel, watching as a few well-heeled guests exit and enter under the same red awning where the four gurneys came rolling out, I can't help dwelling on one of the other strange "coincidences."

My pictures.

Specifically, the transparent effect that happened with the body bags. And then with Penley.

There has to be some logical connection here. . . . But what is it? And does everything in life have to be logical? Since when?

It would be so easy to say that the dream I keep having is a premonition. I never used to believe in that psychic stuff, but now I'm willing to change my mind. *Except the dream already came true.* I saw it with my own eyes. Standing in this exact spot, no less.

The people in those body bags are stone cold dead. Penley—as if I need to be reminded—is very much alive.

Don't go there.

I can't help it, though. The thought creeps into my head, as it's done a few times before. I know it's wrong. I know it's horrible even to think it.

And still, I do.

It's Penley who stands in the way of everything. Were it not for her, I'd have Michael. I'd have Dakota and Sean. I'd have everything I ever wanted.

If only Penley weren't in the picture.

Chapter 51

SERIOUSLY.

Don't. Go. There.

With every step, I try talking myself out of it, but there's another voice, a louder voice — one I barely even recognize as my own — propelling me.

My strides get longer and faster; I'm moving on adrenaline from head to toe. The night air is crisp, a lot cooler than usual for May, and I feel a slight sting on my cheeks.

I look up. *Yes. Of course there's a full moon!*

What should be a ten-minute walk takes only five, and before I know it I'm standing right across the street from Michael's building.

I check my watch. It's a few minutes past midnight.

And you thought you got Michael angry in Connecticut? That was nothing compared to this.

Through the large glass panels flanking the entrance, I can see the night doorman killing time at his desk. I try to remember his name and I'm almost positive it's Adam.

I've only met him once or twice before, when he was filling in on the day shift.

It doesn't matter.

I dial the building's number on my cell phone and watch as he picks up. They always answer the same way, announcing the address in lieu of "Hello."

"Is this Adam?" I ask.

"Yes."

"Hi, it's Kristin, the nanny for the Turnbulls. Listen, I was wondering if you could do me a favor? Louis let me use the staff bathroom off the lobby this morning, and I think I might have left my purse in there. Could you check for me? Sorry."

"Sure, hold on a second."

He puts down the phone and disappears behind the door near his desk. A starter's pistol fires in my head.

Go!

I dart across Fifth Avenue and burst through the front entrance. Racing through the empty lobby, I make it safely to the stairwell before Adam returns.

I'm in.

I hang up my cell and tiptoe up five flights so I'm well out of earshot. Then I call Adam back.

"Sorry to hang up on you; I had another call coming in," I say. "Any luck?"

"No, I'm afraid I didn't see your purse. It's not at the front desk either."

"Darn, I thought that's where I left it. Thanks for looking, though."

"No problem," he says.

That's for sure.

You learn a lot about a building after working in it for

a couple of years. In the case of the Turnbulls', it so happens there are no security cameras on the stairs. *Goody for me.*

Now comes the hard part.

It's called *breaking and entering.*

Chapter 52

I HIKE THE REMAINING thirteen flights, struggling to catch my breath as I reach the penthouse. I check my watch again, which is just a nervous tic, I know.

Lights out at the Turnbulls' is usually no later than ten. Michael rises with the sun, and Penley sees the benefit of a good night's sleep strictly from a cosmetic point of view. God forbid she ever has bags under her eyes.

Still, I cool my heels for another fifteen minutes. One last chance, perhaps, to come to my senses.

The chance passes.

Thumbing through my keys, I find the one Penley gave me when I first began working for her. I distinctly recall her saying something snotty and condescending about it being a symbol of trust. *What, like I'm going to use it to break in one night?*

The key clutched tightly in my hand, I gingerly approach the door and its solid brass lock. Turning my wrist ever so slowly, I try to dull the inevitable *snap* of the dead bolt. It's so quiet around me in the hallway. *Too* quiet. I'm afraid even the slightest noise will wake everyone.

The lock cooperates—barely a sound—and I step inside. I can't see a thing at first. It's pitch-black, but I know the apartment so well it wouldn't matter if I were blindfolded.

This is so insane. What am I doing?

Crossing the foyer, I walk down the long hallway to the bedrooms. Half of me is still pumping with adrenaline, the other half utter fear. It's like I'm on a tightrope without a net. There's no excuse for my being here, at least none that anyone else would understand.

I'm steps away from Dakota's room. I don't intend to go in, and yet that's exactly what I do. I feel the need to look at her, to see her sleeping peacefully, and thanks to the glow of a small heart-shaped night-light by her bed, I can. Nestled under her pink covers, she looks so angelic.

I love Dakota and Sean. Who wouldn't?

Farther down the hallway, I slip into Sean's room. No such luck with a night-light; he doesn't like them.

Squinting, I can barely make out his tiny silhouette in the darkness. I edge closer and closer to him when—*disaster*—I kick something. Legos!

The sound of crashing plastic rips through the room as one of Sean's fantastic creations splatters against a wall.

He stirs and I freeze, holding my breath, my heart thumping out of control.

"Mommy?" he mutters.

Shit.

What now?

I'm about to panic when it comes to me.

"Yes, honey," I whisper. "This is just a dream. . . . Go back to sleep now, okay?"

He seems to think it over for a few agonizing seconds. "Okay," he says finally.

Phew.

I figure if he were really awake he'd recognize my voice. Still, it's a little too close for comfort.

I should take the hint and escape from the apartment as fast as possible. All I have to do is turn left out of Sean's room and never look back.

Instead, I turn right and keep going down the hallway.

To Michael and Penley's room.

Chapter 53

THE DOOR TO MICHAEL and Penley's bedroom is half closed, and there's not enough space for me to squeeze inside. *Here's praying for well-oiled hinges.*

Slowly I push my way in. No squeak. Instead, just the sound of Michael's breathing. It's not quite a snore, more like a low-pitched hum. I recognize it immediately from the few times in which our "sleeping together" actually involved sleeping.

I inch toward them, my footsteps deadened by a huge Persian rug. There's a scant glow of moonlight filtering in through the curtains. As my eyes adjust, I realize what I'm reminded of.

My darkroom.

I stand at the foot of their king-size bed, staring, feeling nervous. Penley's on the left, closer to the bathroom. They're not cuddling, nestling, or spooning—in fact, Michael couldn't be any farther away from her without rolling off the mattress. Nonetheless, the sight of them sharing a bed immediately irks me.

I *know* they're husband and wife, that this is completely normal, even if their marriage isn't. I simply never thought about it this way. I never see any intimacy between the two of them.

Now here I am looking at them together in bed.

What a weird feeling, so uncomfortable, unsettling. It's not so much that I'm jealous. It's more like I'm angry.

I don't think it's possible to hate Penley any more than I do right now, and she hasn't really done anything wrong, has she?

I'm no longer staring at both of them. Just her. I see her bony shoulders jutting out from the puffy duvet, and the turned-up little nose that she wrinkles when something bothers her—which is always. Even asleep she looks like a bitch! Penley could star in *Wicked*—without makeup.

My eyes drift.

Scattered on the bed are more pillows than two people could ever possibly use. I focus on one propped against the headboard, untouched. My brain ignites, and like sparks, the ideas come flying. All of them evil.

How easy it would be to lean over Penley and grab that pillow, place it on her face with my elbows locked and smother her. If I did it quick enough, she wouldn't even struggle, would she? There would be no violent kicking, no muffled screams. She'd die a quick, silent, 100 percent goose down death.

Could I really do it?

Hell, I can't even believe I'm *thinking* it.

It occurs to me: maybe that's the connection—why Penley's picture has the same ghosting effect as the body bags from the Fálcon. It's because *she's in danger*.

From me?

I feel dizzy. A rush of cold air hits me and I gasp, only

to look over at the curtains and see them billowing. The window over the terrace has been open all this time.

A little shiver travels up through my spine and head, jarring my thoughts in an entirely new direction.

I know exactly what I have to do now.

Shoot Michael.

Chapter 54

CAREFULLY, I REMOVE THE LEICA from my shoulder bag, double-checking to make sure it's loaded. My hands steady, I aim right for Michael's head.

Don't think, just shoot.

"Mommy!"

My head whips around. Oh, jeez, it's Sean calling from his room.

"Mommy!" he yells again.

I look back at Michael and Penley. They're waking up. *Quick, hide!*

I glance at my camera. *No, wait. Snap a picture—then hide!*

Sean calls out a third time, his little voice screeching like a siren. He not only sounds louder, he sounds *closer.* Is he out of his bed?

I drop to the floor in a panic. Ten feet away, over by the bathroom, is a small sitting area with a sofa.

I begin crawling toward it on my hands and knees.

I'm completely in the open now. If Penley gets out of

bed, the only way she won't see me is if she trips over me first.

That's when I hear her mumble to Michael, half asleep. It seems she's not going anywhere.

"Go see what he wants," she says.

"He's yelling for his *mommy*," he mumbles back.

"Then let him yell."

Michael groans and pushes back the covers.

Oh no, he's getting out of bed! Michael is going to see me in about two seconds.

The couch is still a few feet away. I scramble to hide behind it. The floorboards creak beneath the rug.

"What was that?" asks Michael.

Penley yawns. "What was *what?*"

"That noise. Didn't you hear? It sounded like it came from inside the room."

I close my eyes. *I'm toast.*

"Mommy?"

I peek out around the sofa. Sean's standing in the doorway now, his voice barely above a whisper.

I'm saved. At least for the moment.

Michael forgets all about the noise in the room. "Hey, what's the matter, little buddy?" he asks.

"I had a bad dream. Dumba came again. Can I sleep in your bed?" Dumba is the monster who sometimes invades Sean's dreams. *Is Dumba maybe the monster who invades my dreams?*

"Sure you can," says Michael. He *is* a nice guy.

"No!" snaps Penley.

"Honey, give the kid a break, will you? He's scared."

"I don't care. He needs to learn that he can't always come running to us."

Michael bristles. "Yeah, and he also needs to learn algebra, but neither has to happen at age five."

As terrified as I am to be stuck there, I can't help thinking, *Good one, Michael!*

Not that Penley would ever be denied. "Fine," she huffs. "I'll give you a choice. If he sleeps in here, you don't!"

"You can't be serious."

"I'm dead serious. You, Sean, and Dumba can go sleep somewhere else."

"Jesus, you're a piece of work, Penley."

I hear Michael's feet land on the floor with a resounding thud. His voice sweetens for Sean. "C'mon, buddy, you and I are sleeping in the guest room."

And off they go.

Leaving me and Penley.

Chapter 55

FOR ONCE I DON'T wake up drenched in sweat and screaming from the dream. *That's because I never go to sleep that night.*

No, I don't hurt Penley, or even say boo to her in their bedroom. I hide behind the sofa, barely moving a muscle, for another hour until I'm convinced it's safe to slip out undetected. Out of the apartment, that is.

Leaving the building is another story.

It's a lot easier to sneak in than it is to sneak out. *Hey, Adam, would you mind looking in the bathroom again for my purse?*

I don't think so.

So I hang out in the stairwell off the penthouse until morning. A new day, a new doorman—and if Louis pauses from his imaginary sword fight with Sean to ask why he didn't see me come in, I'll just joke about him going blind or having Alzheimer's.

I *try* to sleep, Lord knows I'm exhausted enough, but concrete steps make for a lousy pillow. After an hour or so, I give up on the hope of catching any Z's, choosing instead to plan in my head every detail of Michael's and my honeymoon.

The Caribbean? Maybe the Bahamas and the One & Only Ocean Club? Venice and the Gritti Palace? The French Riviera?

All I know is that when we get back, Sean can sleep in our bed whenever he wants. In fact, maybe for our honeymoon we'll take the kids to Disney World. Why not?

At about five-fifteen, I hear the first signs of life on the other side of the stairwell door. It's Michael leaving for his office. *Five-fifteen?* That's even earlier than usual. I suppose that's what a night in the guest room will do to you.

At about a quarter to eight, it's my turn. For the second day in a row, I'm early for work. If I keep it up, I might just get a raise!

I let myself into the apartment. Again.

"*My,* someone looks tired," says Penley with an obnoxious grin as I greet her in the kitchen. "You must have had a late night." *Wink-wink, nudge-nudge.*

It takes me a second to catch her drift. My blind date with Stephen seems like a week ago, or like it didn't even happen.

"I want *all* the details," she insists.

I'm too tired and in no mood, especially because there isn't much to tell. "He was very nice," I say.

Penley frowns, then she shakes her head. "You're going to have to do better than that, Kristin."

I thought as much. So I ply her with some mindless details about the dinner, and while I don't come right out and say it, I make it clear that her gym friend is not "my type." For sure, I don't want her pushing for a second date.

Then she surprises me. "Yeah, Stephen pretty much felt the same way."

"You spoke to him already?"

"Hope you don't mind," she says with a shrug. "He's a friend, after all, and I was curious."

I can see that.

She turns and pours herself another steaming cup of coffee, which looks delicious, by the way. One day she might actually ask if I want one.

"You know, Stephen got the sense that you were already seeing someone."

Thanks, pal!

"I tried to assure him I'm not," I say. "It's a little funny to hear that, though, given he still seems hung up on his ex-girlfriend."

"You think so?"

"Absolutely. Did you know she's a married woman, by the way?"

Her eyes go wide. *Apparently not.*

"He neglected to mention that," she says with a smirk. "I apologize."

Penley? Apologizing?

"For what?" I ask.

"Thinking Stephen was right for you. I don't approve of that sort of thing. He should know better," she says, frowning. "Don't you agree?"

Oh, the irony.

Chapter 56

I STRUGGLE TO STAY awake while I walk the kids to school. I've got one eye just about closed, the other trained on Dakota, as I still wonder what's going through her mind.

Indeed, she wasn't quite herself yesterday, spending most of the time in her room. Her daddy and I were only talking behind those hedges out in Westport, but the whole vibe of the moment must have seemed a little less than innocent. Eventually, I take Dakota's hand in mine, and she lets me.

"Hey, Miss Kristin, guess what?" chirps Sean as we march across the street at Madison and 76th. "You were in my dream last night!"

Oh, great . . . *double trouble*.

For the last couple of blocks before Preston Academy, I listen to Sean explaining his dream in great detail. Apparently he and I had a picnic on the moon.

"Or was it Mars?" he wonders.

The details are a little fuzzy, but what's clear is that he has no recollection of my being in his room. *Hallelujah. One less thing to worry about.*

That leaves only about a dozen others. What's bumming me out the most, I think, is that after all I went through last night, I wasn't able to snap a shot of Michael. I was so spooked by nearly getting caught that all I could think about was escaping from the apartment as soon as possible.

"Okay, my angels," I say, kneeling just outside the gates of Preston Academy. "Have a wonderful day, listen to your teachers, and I'll be here this afternoon to pick you up."

"Bye," says Sean, and he kisses me on the cheek.

"Thanks," says Dakota. "Just for being nice."

As always, I watch their mad dash to join their friends and head inside the school. When Sean falls behind, Dakota stops and sticks out her hand, patiently waiting. My heart sighs.

It's settled. Michael and I are definitely taking them to Disney World for our honeymoon!

I turn and head back toward Fifth Avenue, a different song—finally—playing in my head. "It's a small world after all. . . ."

Less than a block later, my cell phone rings. What's this?

Serendipity! It's Michael. I knew it was only a matter of time before he called.

"I was just thinking of you," I say.

"Not as much as I've been thinking of you, Kris. I've missed you so much!"

Before I can say ditto, he apologizes.

"For what?" I ask. "That's what I should be doing. I'm *so* sorry for what I did. I'm mortified."

"No, it was wrong of me to cancel on you. Penley is such a bitch," he says. "I should've never gone out to Westport."

"That makes two of us."

We laugh, and he simply couldn't be any sweeter. It doesn't take long for me to make the connection to the rotten night he had sleeping with Sean and Dumba in the guest room. If only he knew I saw it all firsthand.

It's amazing, really. For everything I've said and done as part of my Dump Penley campaign, my efforts are no match for Penley herself. At this rate, Michael might even dump her by the Fourth of July.

Independence Day.

What fireworks that would be!

"I've got another business dinner this evening," says Michael, "but I want to make sure we're together tomorrow night. Anything you want, we'll do it, okay?"

"You've got yourself a date," I answer.

"God, I'm so lucky to have you."

"Don't you forget it!"

We say good-bye, laced with *I love you*s, and I put my cell phone away. Opening my shoulder bag, I see that the lens cap has fallen off my camera. As I snap it back on, I notice something else.

I loaded a new roll of film before sneaking into Michael and Penley's apartment last night. Since I didn't snap a single picture, the shot counter should still read 0.

Only it reads 1.

Chapter 57

MAYBE THE CAMERA JOSTLED in my bag, triggering the shutter. It could happen. Especially these days.

But there's another possibility. . . .

The thought immediately spins me around. Now I'm walking in the opposite direction.

Out comes my cell phone again, and I call Penley. Actually, I call her answering machine, since I know she's still at the gym. Not that she'd pick up anyway.

A filling just fell out, I explain. Luckily, my dentist can take me right away. "Don't worry, I'll be done in plenty of time to pick up the kids at three."

That takes care of that. Next stop: my darkroom.

I've never burned an entire roll of film for only one picture, but if there's going to be a first time, this is definitely it.

I have to see 1.

Right before Sean called out last night, I had Michael lined up in my lens. Maybe —*just maybe* — I managed to get the shot without even knowing it.

The desire to find out takes over, and I'm quickly

hailing a cab in lieu of walking. I'm riding another wave of adrenaline, my mind and body oblivious to the fact that I've been awake for over twenty-four hours. And counting.

"Keep the change," I tell the cabbie, dropping seven bucks in his lap as he pulls up to my building. Less than a minute later, I'm alone in my darkroom, the main light out and the door closed. The safety is on and everything is eerily red in the small room.

I'm getting pretty good at speed developing lately, and with this roll of film, I set a new record. My eyes and hands are in complete sync—reaching, pouring, setting, shifting—everything it takes to bring this one picture to life.

What if it's not Michael?

It could be anything, really. Maybe it's Penley. Or nothing at all.

A blur, a blob, or complete blackness. Perhaps all I've got is a glitch in the camera's shot counter, and this supposed picture doesn't even exist.

If that's the case, I'll have to be patient. I'll wait until tomorrow night when Michael and I are together and snap a shot of him then. After all, it's only another day to wait.

I glare at the processing tank. "Hurry up, you lazy-ass film!"

Then again, I'm not exactly in a patient mood.

I anxiously tap my fingers, waiting for the first sign of an image. Gradually, one appears.

I shift the negative over to the holding bath and lean in for a better view. It's someone, but I can't be sure who. So I hurriedly make a print, and that's when I know.

It's Michael, all right. I did take a picture of him after all.

And as I look closely at the shot, I see what I didn't want to see—the same ghosting effect I noticed with Penley.

"Shit. Don't do this."

But there's something else, something even more bizarre.

Scary is more like it. Terrifying!

I immediately plunge a hand into the cold water of the holding bath, grabbing the shot while reaching for my magnifying loupe.

Oh, my God, Michael. What have I done?

He isn't lying in bed beside Penley. He's sprawled on the floor of a room I don't recognize. A place I don't believe I've ever been in my life.

And he looks *dead*.

Chapter 58

IT'S AS IF THE PHOTOGRAPH literally shocks me, sending a thousand volts of instant pain through my fingertips. It drops from my hands, landing facedown on the floor.

Like Michael.

I step back, terrified. How? What? Where? *When?* I don't have a single answer to any of these questions. *What's real? What isn't?* There has to be a rational explanation. That's what I've been saying all along, beginning with the dream. But looking at this picture of Michael, I don't know. *How do you explain the inexplicable?*

I don't.

At least not yet.

Back and forth I pace in the tight confines of my darkroom, repeating the same four words over and over in my head.

Keep it together, Kris!

I figure I've got two choices. Check myself into the loony bin or continue chipping away at this mystery. I stop pacing as the image of a padded room and me wearing the latest style in straitjackets flashes through my mind.

Decision made.

I rush out to the kitchen and pick up the phone. If I can't explain the picture of Michael, there's still the issue of the ghosting effect. On the heels of everything else, I'm thinking it has nothing to do with my camera. But I need to make sure.

"Gotham Photo," the man answers.

"Hi, can I speak with Javier, please? It's kind of important." *Like, life and death.*

"He's off today."

Damn. "Do you know how I can reach him?"

"Afraid I don't."

There's a slight hitch in his voice, and I suspect he does know.

"It's *very* important," I say.

"We're not allowed to give out personal information. The best I can do is relay a message to him, okay?"

No, not okay!

I'm about to launch into the kind of full-frontal "helpless female in distress" plea that would make Gloria Steinem gag when I remember my closet. Thanks to a few cockroaches—give or take a thousand—I never checked the pockets of my shearling coat for Javier's cell number.

"Hold on a second, will you?" I say.

I drop the phone, dash to the closet, and pray that my existential exterminator knew what he was doing with that poison spray.

I slowly open the door to see only coats—including my shearling. Chalk one up for my memory; Javier's card is right where I thought.

"Never mind," I say, returning to the phone. *Click.*

The second I get a dial tone, I call Javier. It's such a relief when he answers.

"I'm so sorry to bother you, Javier."

"Don't worry about it," he says. I'm sure he likes me and I feel a little guilty about this.

I remind him about the "ghosting" effect. "Remember? I mentioned it when I bought the new lens."

"So the problem wasn't with your old one, huh?"

"Afraid not. I know it's your day off, but would you mind taking a look at the pictures? I really need to figure this out."

"That depends," he says.

"On what?"

"On how well you know your way around Brooklyn."

Chapter 59

NOT VERY WELL.

In fact, the closest I've ever been to Brooklyn is watching reruns of *Welcome Back, Kotter* on Nick at Nite.

But after picking up the kids at school and pretending all afternoon that my mouth is still sore from the dentist, I board the F train heading out of Manhattan and hope for the best.

I generally don't mind riding the subway, except for rush hour, when it's a madhouse.

Of course, that happens to be *right now.*

Wedged in with a gazillion other people—including the guy hovering next to me whose twenty-four-hour deodorant is clearly living on borrowed time—I'm afraid the old adage is wrong. Getting there is not half the fun.

But at least I get there, and thanks to Javier's very precise directions from the 15th Street–Prospect Park station, I easily find the nearby brownstone where he lives.

It's a pretty nice neighborhood, and I can't help feeling a bit guilty about my low expectations, if not outright trepidation. I hate those people who think the good life begins and ends in the 212 area code, and here I am acting like one.

Javier's apartment occupies the first floor, and he greets me at the door with his usual warm smile. He's dressed much the same as when he's behind the counter at Gotham Photo—khakis and a button-down shirt, in this case a blue-and-white stripe. The only thing missing is his name tag.

"Can I offer you something to drink?" he asks.

"A Diet Coke, if you have one."

He does. I follow him back to the kitchen, stealing quick peeks into some of the rooms.

I see a beautifully furnished den with a huge flat-screen television and a cozy library lined with leather-bound books. It's not what I expected, and again I feel like one of those 212 snobs. How fitting that selling camera equipment to those same people would apparently pay so well.

He pours the soda into a glass with ice and hands it to me. "Now let's take a look at those pictures," he says. "Figure out what's going on."

"Excellent."

I reach into my shoulder bag and pull them out. He's barely had a chance to look at the first one when I realize . . . we're not alone.

Chapter 60

"JAVIER?" COMES A VOICE from another room. "Javier? Is someone there with you?" It's a woman. She sounds old, foreign, and a bit confused.

"Sí, Mamá," says Javier over his shoulder. He turns back to me. "My mother moved in last year after my father passed away. Unfortunately, her health is not too good."

"Javier?" she calls out again. "I'm talking to you. Javier?"

He winks at me. "Her hearing isn't too good either." He raises his voice. "Sí, Mamá!"

"Con quién estás hablando?"

Javier translates for me. "She wants to know who I'm talking to." He answers her, "Ella es mi amiga."

"La has visto antes?"

He rolls his eyes. "She wants to know if she's met you before. Now I have to introduce you, otherwise she'll be offended. Do you mind? I'm sorry."

"Don't be," I say. "I'd love to meet her."

Javier leads me out of the kitchen toward the very back

of the apartment. He slows for a moment along the narrow hallway to whisper something to me.

"Just so you know, my mother is very religious and she's gone a little overboard in her decorating."

I'm not sure why he's telling me this. That is, until we reach her room.

Jesus!

Literally. There have to be at least a hundred crucifixes hanging on the wall—big, small, wood, ceramic—with another fifty propped up on a bookshelf and bedside table.

"Mamá, ella es mi amiga Kristin."

She's sitting in a rocking chair by the window, wearing the plainest of plain tank dresses—*cement gray,* if I had to name the color. But what I really notice is how incredibly frail she looks. She's so thin she'd give Penley a fat complex.

As she glares at me with sunken eyes, I walk toward her and extend my hand. It seems like the right thing to do.

Wrong.

Terribly wrong!

I get no farther than a few steps when those sunken eyes explode with fear. She clutches a set of blue rosary beads in her lap and begins to scream wildly. All hell breaks loose in this claustrophobic room full of crosses.

"Espíritus malos! Espíritus malos! Mantengase lejos de mí. Ella está poseída por espíritus malos!"

Javier gasps. "Mamá! *What are you saying?*"

That's what I want to know, but Javier isn't translating. Instead, he rushes to her, trying to calm her down. She doesn't.

She gets worse, in fact, more crazed and agitated.

"Ella está rodeada por espíritus malos!" she screams, her sliver of a body nearly out of control.

Javier grabs her and yells something in Spanish, but it's as if she can't see or hear him. She keeps pointing and hollering.

At me.

"Espíritus malos! Espíritus malos!"

Javier's worried face leaves little doubt that this is something his mother has never done before. "I'm sorry, Kristin, but I think it's best if you leave."

"Espíritus malos! Espíritus malos!" the old woman shrieks. She's also stamping her feet on the floor.

"What does she keep saying?" I ask, as I slowly back out of the room.

"It's nonsense," says Javier. "Don't worry about it."

"No, I want to know. *Tell me.*"

His mother begins to convulse, her rocking chair now like an electric chair. She bites down so hard on her lower lip that blood begins to trickle. My God!

"Mamá!" yells Javier.

The old woman is jabbing her finger at me.

"Espíritus malos! Espíritus malos!"

"Kristin, I'll look at your pictures another time. At work. You really need to leave!"

But I can't yet. "Not until you tell me what she's saying. I have to know!"

He glares at me, clearly vexed at my persistence, if not my presence.

"C'mon, Javier, tell me!" I plead.

Finally, he does.

"Espíritus malos," he says. "My mother says you're possessed by evil spirits. She thinks you're a devil."

Chapter 61

I'M SO DIZZY leaving Javier's apartment I nearly do a face plant on the sidewalk. I stagger for a block or so, shaking my head.

What on earth just happened? I'm a devil? Me?

The image of his mother keeps repeating in my mind, her screams echoing in my ears. *Espíritus malos! Espíritus malos!*

Again I tell myself to keep it together.

For the first time I'm not sure I can.

Espíritus malos . . . I'm a devil.

Of all the questions I have, I realize there's now another. *Where am I?*

I've been walking, oblivious to the unfamiliar streets or even the direction I'm heading. It's almost dusk.

I stop and rummage through my shoulder bag, pushing aside the pictures I remembered to grab on the way out. Next I check my pockets, but they're not there either. Javier's directions are nowhere to be found.

Oh, great. I'm lost in Brooklyn.

"Excuse me," I say to the next person I pass, a young

woman with a backpack. She can't be more than twenty. "Do you know where I can find the F train?"

She barely slows down. "Sorry, I'm not from around here."

You and me both.

Farther down the block I see an older man, perhaps in his seventies, sitting on a stoop reading the *Daily News.* He looks sort of like Ernest Borgnine.

"The F train, huh?" He points over my shoulder. "The first thing you want to do is turn around."

I do exactly that as he begins to rattle off the lefts and rights I need to take. I'm listening as best I can, trying to keep track. *Did he say two lefts before the right or one?*

I'm about to ask him to repeat everything when I see something I don't want to see.

Some*one,* actually. A man.

It may be dusk, but I can see him clear as day. That's what having darkroom eyes will do for you.

I wait a second, and again he pokes his head out from behind the white delivery truck double-parked at the corner. I don't even need to see the face.

All it takes is the ponytail.

Chapter 62

"HEY, LADY, YOU'RE GOING the wrong way again!" growls the old man on the stone stoop.

Not as far as I'm concerned. Lost in Brooklyn is one thing. *Killed* is another.

I'm not quite running. It's more like speed walking. Nervously, I glance over my shoulder, my eyes scanning the entire street.

I don't see the Ponytail now, and that only scares me more because I'm sure—*really* sure—it's him again. Does he want to give me another warning? *Or are we out of warnings?*

I turn a corner and I'm picking up speed. What I need to find is a cop or someone big enough to protect me. Better yet, someone bulletproof. But there's no help to be found. All I can see is a deserted street, lined with warehouses and heaps of trash.

Is the Ponytail behind me? I look back again, staring hard at the corner.

I don't see him anywhere coming after me. Not yet, anyway.

The shadows are disappearing, though. Not good news. It's getting darker by the second.

I keep looking until eventually I'm standing still in the middle of the block. I'm waiting and waiting. *Where is he? What does he want with me?*

Maybe he took off. Like, for some reason he didn't want me to see him this time.

A minute passes. Then another. It's officially night. I can barely make out the corner anymore. The only available light is a streetlamp at the next intersection. With one last glance over my shoulder, I head that way. I still need directions. I'm *still* lost in Brooklyn.

Then I see it.

A taxi!

It creeps to a stop at the red light hovering over the crosswalk. Twenty feet away—thirty tops. I can hear the engine rumbling.

Hurry! Before the light turns green!

I break into a sprint, my eyes locked on the taxi, desperately willing it not to move.

With one last surge, I close the gap to a few steps. I wave my arms again and shout, "Taxi! Taxi!" There's no way the cabbie can miss me.

Or so I think.

The light turns green, and the taxi lurches forward. "No!" I yell. "Wait! Hey, stop!"

It doesn't. I'm steps away, and it's about to pass right in front of me.

Over my dead body!

I jump right into its path. The cabbie slams on the brakes, the screech of bald tires piercing the air. By the time the substantial chrome bumper rocks to a halt, it's inches from my kneecaps.

Ignoring the cabbie's evil eye, I stomp around to climb into the backseat. But when I reach for the door, out of nowhere comes another hand.

"Allow me," he says.

Chapter 63

BEFORE I CAN RUN, the Ponytail grabs my arm with an iron grip. Then he swings open the taxi door and roughly shoves me in. I tumble onto the seat, and he slides in right next to me. I'm trapped!

"Shhh," he immediately whispers, pulling back the lapel on his black sport coat. There's barely any light, but I can still see it. *His gun.*

Through the Plexiglas divider, I spot the cabbie—a stocky bald guy like that actor on *The Shield*—glaring at me in his rearview mirror. "You're lucky I didn't run you over," he says. "I almost hit you."

"Sorry about that," I answer while glancing at the Ponytail. "Finding a taxi around here can be murder."

The Ponytail grips my arm again, even tighter. *Ow!* He leans in, close to my ear. "Don't get cute. There's nothing funny about this, believe me."

"Where you headed?" asks the cabbie. "I'm not a mind reader, y'know."

"Just drive," says the Ponytail. "Stay in the general area. But drive."

The cabbie flips the meter on and shrugs as if to say, "Hey, it's your dime."

And off we go.

I look over at my backseat companion. I don't want to show fear, but I shudder anyway. His narrow, sharp-featured face is menacing up close. I see a scar beneath the three-day stubble on his cheek. I suspect it's the kind you don't get by "accident." Why is he following me? Is he a cop? Is this about what happened at the Fálcon?

The cabbie fiddles with the radio, turning the volume up on a jazz station.

As scared as I am, there's a part of me almost emboldened by the idea that my fate is seemingly out of my hands. I've got my Bronx up. Or, I should say, my Brooklyn.

"Who are you?" I ask.

"Your worst nightmare," the Ponytail answers, his voice a deep baritone. No accent that I can decipher.

"That's a very crowded category these days."

"Serves you right," he says. "You did this to yourself."

"What's that supposed to mean?"

"You've been a bad girl, Kristin. You must know that. You deserve what you're getting. And it's going to get worse."

Another shudder goes through me. "How do you know my name?"

"Trust me; I know a lot more about you than just your name. I know when you moved down here from Boston and why. I know where you live and where you work."

The conversation flows like the jazz on the radio. Fast and choppy. Also random. *Where's the Ponytail going with this?*

Right for my jugular, it turns out.

"Do you love those two kids?" he asks. "Those cute little kids?"

Sean and Dakota?

"What does this have to do with them?"

"Everything, I expect. Those kids are very important in all this."

"Don't you dare hurt them," I snap at him, and raise a fist.

"No," he says. "Don't *you* dare hurt them."

"Ha! You're wrong, then," I say. "You don't know anything about me."

The volume dips abruptly on the radio. "Everything okay back there?" asks the cabbie.

It's clearly not a courtesy question. There's a note of suspicion and alarm in his voice. He can probably tell something's wrong.

I don't want to get this driver killed, but I know about the "panic button"—most every New Yorker does. It triggers a light on the back of the taxi that signals to police that something's wrong, like a robbery or carjacking in progress.

Or whatever this is.

How do I tip off the driver to push the panic button without getting caught?

The Ponytail clears his throat. He's not about to let me figure that out.

"Everything's fine," he announces.

The cabbie seeks out my eyes in his mirror. "Are you sure, lady?" he asks. "Everything's fine?"

The Ponytail whispers fast and forcefully in my ear. The way he's squeezing my arm really hurts. "Tell him to mind his own business."

I take a deep breath and sigh. "We're okay," I say. "No need to panic."

I don't know if the cabbie gets the hint, but the Pony-tail sure does.

Dumb move, Kris!

"I told you not to get cute," he says, reaching inside his coat. "How many times do you have to be warned?"

Chapter 64

THE PONYTAIL'S GOING to kill me. Right now, right here. That's what this is. Everything's been leading up to my death, my murder.

The thought seems to reach every nerve ending in my body at once. All of a sudden I'm shaking all over.

But it's not a gun that comes out of his jacket. It's his wallet.

"Stop the cab!" barks the Ponytail.

He pulls out twenty bucks and pushes the money through the slot in the divider as the taxi swerves over to the curb. It happens so fast.

"Consider this your last warning, Kristin," he says. "Go home and pack your things. Move out of town. Disappear from the Turnbull family before it's too late."

"Too late for what?" I ask.

"I think you already know. There are four people involved, Kristin. Don't hurt them!"

He steps out of the taxi, slamming the door hard behind him. He stares at me through the side window. Murmurs a few words. I'm pretty sure the last one is *warned*.

"Friend of yours?" says the cabbie sarcastically.

"JUST GO!" I yell. "PLEASE, GO! GO!"

He hits the gas and we take off, those bald tires screeching again.

I spin around and gaze out the rear window as the Ponytail stands there watching me. He starts to blend into the night until all I can see is the white of his teeth. He's smiling a sick grin.

There are four people. . . . Don't hurt them.

Chapter 65

CONSIDER THIS your last warning, Kristin.

But who's warning me?

And why?

Somebody from the police? Is Detective Delmonico involved?

"So are we actually *going* somewhere?" asks the cabbie, interrupting my manic train of thought.

"Manhattan," I answer. "Please."

I barely manage to give him my address before sinking down in the seat, ready to pass out. I've been awake for a day and a half. I'd almost find it funny if I had the energy to laugh anymore.

"Hey, you sure you're okay back there, lady?"

"Yeah," I lie. "Just another day at the beach."

Any mild relief I'm feeling is squashed by my lingering fear. *It's as if he's still sitting next to me, warning me about the Turnbull family.*

I'm shivering and feeling dizzy. What's more, my body is one big itch. Hives again? Whatever it is, I'm scratching all over like mad.

In fact, it's going from bad to worse. I feel as if my skin's crawling. *What's going on with me?*

We pass a streetlamp, the backseat filling with a hazy yellow glow. I quickly push up my sleeve to look at my arm. I expect to see bright red from all the scratching.

Instead I see something else. *Something is moving!*

I jolt up in the seat as the rear of the taxi goes dark again. I'm swatting at my arm, at what exactly, I don't know. But I definitely feel something.

"What the hell are you doing?" asks the cabbie, surely wishing he *had* run me over at this point.

"There's something on me!" I shout.

He flips the overhead light on. I immediately see it and scream my head off. It's a cockroach . . . except it's not on me.

It's *in* me.

The thing is crawling under my skin, the ghastly shape unmistakable—legs, body, antennae—marching up toward my elbow. I keep striking myself, beating my arm.

Then I see another roach and another after that, forcing their way beneath my flesh. And what I can't see, I feel. In my legs, my stomach, my face. The cockroaches are everywhere!

I'm thrashing in the backseat, my arms flailing. *I have to get out of this taxi!* But as I reach for the door, the locks snap down. At least I think that's what just happened. I pull in vain on the handle. I'm trapped.

"UNLOCK THE DOOR!" I yell at the cabbie, but he doesn't. Maybe because I've succeeded in scaring the hell out of him.

Up ahead, I see the brick wall of a building getting close in a hurry. It's a dead end in the worst sense of the word.

I can't bear to look at this. I close my eyes and cover my face with my arm.

Then *WHACK! BAM! CRASH!* As though my life is a cartoon.

Everything goes black.

Chapter 66

"WHAT'S THE NAME of this hospital?" I ask the thirty-something doctor as he looks up from the clipboard in his lap.

"Our Lady of Hope," he answers.

"And how did I get here again?"

"A cabdriver dropped you off. He said you started screaming in his backseat so he slammed on the brakes. That's when you hit your head on the divider. Apparently, it knocked you out."

Dr. Curley, as his name tag reads, squints at my hairline. "Now, are you sure I can't get you some more ice for that nasty bump?" he asks.

"No," I say. "I'm okay."

But I'm clearly not, and he knows it. The nurses and doctors in the emergency room were quick to grasp it too. All it took was five minutes of my rambling on about bizarre photographs, devils, a recurring dream, the Ponytail, and subdermal cockroaches before the consensus concern for my head officially had nothing to do with the nasty bump on it.

*Kristin, say hello to Dr. Curley—our staff psychia-
trist here at the hospital.*

I'm sitting across from him in a small office near the
waiting room. There's no desk, no pictures on the wall,
no phone—just two folding chairs. Cozy.

"You think I'm crazy, don't you?" I ask.

Dr. Curley, a warm and fuzzy type with a mop of long-
ish blond hair, taps his pen a few times on his clipboard
before shrugging. "Do *you* think you're crazy?"

"I must be if they called you down here to see me.
Don't you think so?"

"Don't read too much into that." He leans in as if sharing a secret. "Between you and me, the hospital is usually just trying to get their money's worth from having a
shrink on staff. And they like to protect their butts."

"Though I suppose I can't blame them in my case," I say.

He glances down at the notes he's been taking. He certainly seems nicer than my ex-therapist, Dr. Corey, and
from what I can tell, he doesn't smoke a ridiculous pipe.

"Well, you've definitely had an eventful week," he says,
looking up again with a reassuring smile. "I'd like to try
something if you don't mind. Won't take long, I promise."

I listen to him explain his "simple exercise." All I have
to do is fill in the blank.

"For example," he says, "I consider myself a *blank*
person. And you would answer . . . ?"

Nothing.

I sit there like a lump. "It sure would be easier if this
were multiple choice," I say, stalling, trying to figure out
what the game is here and if I really want to play.

He chuckles. "I suppose you're right. Just remember there are no wrong answers, so don't overthink it.

All I ask is that you be as honest with your answers as possible."

"Because there are no wrong answers," I say.

"That's right."

He repeats the sentence for me. *I consider myself a . . .*

"Decent person," I answer.

"See? Nothing to it. Okay, next one," he says, picking up the pace. "The world is getting more *blank*."

"Dangerous," I say. No indecision about that one.

"I think most people are . . ."

"Lonely."

"When I'm under stress I like to . . ."

"Work in my darkroom."

"If I could change one thing about myself it would be . . ."

"My career. I mean, I'd like to be more successful at it. I'm a photographer."

"The last person I got upset at was . . ."

"Myself."

"The most important person in my life is . . ."

Without thinking, I open my mouth to answer "Michael." I barely catch myself. *I can't tell him that!*

"What's wrong?" asks Dr. Curley.

"Uh, nothing," I say, shifting in my seat. "I had to think about it for a second. The most important person in my life is Connie, my best friend."

He nods. He's been nodding all along, only this one is a little different, slower. *Does he know I'm lying? Of course he does. The guy's no dummy.*

"Okay, last two," he says. "I had a *blank* childhood."

I hesitate before answering. "Difficult."

"And last, the thing I'm most afraid of is . . ."

That's easy. "Dying."

Chapter 67

I WATCH AS Dr. Curley makes a few more quick notes, his pen gliding back and forth across his notepad. Given my lack of sleep, the effect is like the swinging pocket watch of a hypnotist. I can barely keep my eyes open. *But I do not want the dream to come again!*

"Still with me, Kristin?"

I snap to. The pen's down, and he's staring at me. "Yes. Sorry about that," I say.

"Quite all right. No problem."

"So, did I pass?"

"Like I said, there are no wrong answers. No trick ones either. But I do appreciate your honesty."

"What now?" I ask. *Speaking of honesty.*

He adjusts his wire-rimmed glasses. "Here's what I'm thinking," he begins. "It's getting late, you're miles from home, you've suffered a minor concussion, and you're clearly exhausted. How would you feel about spending the night here at the hospital?"

When you put it that way . . .

The thought of not having to make the trip back to

Manhattan immediately appeals to me *so much*. So does the prospect of—at long last—a good night's sleep. Who knows? Maybe being in a hospital will stave off that damn dream, the burning smell, the bug thing.

"Sure, why not?" I say.

Dr. Curley tells me to "hang out and relax" for a moment, as he needs to clear it with another doctor. He leaves, closing the door behind him.

I sit and wait. I'm getting a little bit antsy now. And paranoid? Of course.

A few minutes go by, followed by a few more. I'm hanging out, but I'm definitely not relaxing. *Where is he? C'mon, c'mon. I'm clearly exhausted, remember?*

I get up from the chair and walk to the door, opening it just enough to poke my head out. Sure enough, I spot Dr. Curley down the hall, talking on his cell phone. He's standing with another man, who I assume is the doctor he mentioned. But I can't quite see him thanks to Curley's bushy blond hair.

Then Dr. Curley shifts his feet, and I manage to catch a glimpse of the other doctor's face. I immediately do a double take, and my heart does a little flip-flop. Make that a big flip-flop.

I know him!

Or at least I used to.

Before he was murdered in my hometown of Concord, Massachusetts.

Chapter 68

THIS IS A MONSTER CLUE in the ongoing mystery called "my life of late." It has to be.

I whip my head back from the hallway, quickly shutting the door. I'm alone in the room and *desperately* want to keep it that way.

I have no idea how Dr. Magnumsen, my pediatrician from my hometown, could be alive, let alone working in Brooklyn. What's more, he hasn't aged a day. He looks exactly as he did when I last saw him.

Back when I was twelve years old.

The doubts creep in like a heavy fog. Is it really him? Maybe this doctor just looks like Floyd Magnumsen. Right down to the cleft chin?

I know one way to find out. *Walk right up and ask.* If I'm right, he won't even have to answer. Given the past—why and how he was killed—the look on his face will say it all.

Christ, listen to yourself, Kristin! If you're right, that means you'll be talking to a dead man!

And if I'm wrong? If I go into that hallway and make another insane scene?

Suffice to say, the hospital will put me up in a room, all right. One with wall-to-wall padding. And a little window so they can watch me at all times.

But it's Magnumsen; I know it is.

Like I know I saw my father. I even have the pictures to prove it.

Wait. *Pictures!*

I rush over to my shoulder bag and grab my camera, checking for film. It's ready.

Am I? And for what? The next test?

I pause by the door, swallowing hard, my cheek resting against the cool wood. I need to be quick and I need to be quiet. I can't let anyone see me take the shot. Not Dr. Curley, and especially not Magnumsen. *Why is that, Kris? Because the dead don't like having their pictures taken?*

Carefully, I peek into the hallway again. The two men are still together, but Dr. Curley and his blond hair have moved again, blocking my shot.

Camera raised, I watch through my lens, waiting for the Kodak moment. *C'mon, Doc, move a little!*

He doesn't. The man's a statue.

Which means I am too. How long can I stand here before someone—

Now!

For a split second, Dr. Curley shifts his feet as he tucks away his cell phone. I've got the shot! More proof that I'm not a mad person, just that the world has gone mad all around me. Makes sense—if you're in my shoes, anyway.

Right as I snap the pic, I hear a scream over my shoulder. I spin to see a very pregnant woman hunched over at the entrance to the emergency room. She screams again, and two nurses rush toward her.

She's pointing at the room I'm in — looking and pointing right at me.

She screams again and utters just one word: *"Satan!"*

And she's not the only one looking my way. So is Dr. Magnumsen.

If I wasn't sure before, I am now. It's been nearly fifteen years, but it's as if I haven't aged a day either. This man who molested me — my pediatrician — recognizes who I am in an instant.

The wretched look on his face says it all.

Chapter 69

"KRISTIN, PLEASE unlock the door," says Dr. Robert Curley in the perfect tone for reading Dr. Seuss to preschoolers.

I don't. I don't even respond to this complete fraud.

"Whatever's bothering you, I'm sure we can help." *Did you say "we," Robbie?*

I hear the strain in his voice as he tries to remain warm and fuzzy. There must be a book somewhere, *How to Talk to a Nutcase*. Lesson one: Never, ever lose your cool.

"C'mon, Kristin, I'm not the enemy," he says.

It's an interesting choice of words, and I speak up.

"Is he with you?" I ask. "Is he still out there?"

"Is who with me?"

Ha! I know Floyd Magnumsen is standing right there; I can feel it. Why is Robbie playing dumb now, I wonder? Unless, of course, he's part of all this.

I fall silent again, listening as Curley repeatedly tries to coax me out of this tiny box of a room. It's no use, and he knows it. His frustration mounts, and soon warm and fuzzy turn to piss and vinegar.

"JUST OPEN THE DOOR!" he yells. "OPEN IT THIS INSTANT."

Curley begins pounding the door with his fist. I keep my eyes glued on the knob with its push-button lock, terrified that it might pop out from all the rattling.

"YOU CAN'T STAY IN THERE FOREVER!"

We'll see about that.

The shouting and pounding stop, quickly replaced by whispering. I press my ear against the door. Magnumsen is talking. I can barely make out what he's saying, but what I do hear is enough.

"The key. Who has the key? We have to get her out of there."

Immediately, I grab one of the chairs and try to wedge it under the doorknob. It's not tall enough. *Now what?*

Although I may be desperate, I'm not stupid. I won't be able to hold off Curley and Magnumsen once they have the key.

But I know someone who can.

My hands trembling, I dial a number on my cell. I've got *one* bar of signal, and it's flashing in and out. Through bursts of static, the line rings once, then twice.

On the third ring, I hear footsteps out in the hallway followed by a key sliding into the lock.

Pick up! Pick up! Pick up!

The door flies open, smacking against the wall. I don't see Magnumsen. Dr. Curley immediately grabs for the phone, but I won't let go. I'm clinging to my cell like a pit bull when I hear another *pop* of static and the voice I've been waiting for.

"Hello?"

I scream the name of the hospital as Curley and I fall to the ground in a tug-of-war. One by one, he begins prying my fingers loose. It hurts like hell.

"Help, Michael, you have to save me!"

Chapter 70

"ARE THE DOORS LOCKED?" I whisper. "You checked?"

"Yes."

"Are you absolutely sure? I *know* I sound a little crazy right now."

Michael reaches for a button on the ceiling of the limo and lowers the tinted-glass divider halfway. "Vin, the doors are locked, right?"

"Yes, sir," grunts Vincent. But just to be nice, Vincent unlocks and locks them again.

Up goes the divider with a mechanical hum. Michael and I are in our own little world again. I'm lying across the backseat with my head in his lap as he gently caresses the nasty bump below my hairline. That bump is *real*. So is the rest of what happened. "Everything's going to be okay," he assures me.

What I wouldn't give for him to be right. For the time being, though, I'll take being out of that hospital.

"I didn't think that awful jerk Curley would ever release me," I say.

Michael nods. "He was pretty stubborn, wasn't he?"

"What did you say to make him change his mind?"

"Oh, nothing, really. I simply suggested that since you came to the emergency room voluntarily, you should also leave that way."

"That's it? That's all you said?"

Michael flashes his trademark smile. "Well, I did mention one other thing."

I knew it.

"I told him that by the time I was done suing Our Lady of Hope Hospital for false imprisonment, it would be renamed Our Lady of Bankruptcy."

That's the man I love.

Michael doesn't press me for details on what happened, and as much as I want to tell him, I'm torn. He just came to my rescue and vouched for my sanity. If I try explaining everything right now, what's he supposed to think? I'm afraid he'll tell Vincent to turn the limo around: "Quick, let's get her back to the hospital!"

Besides, I don't want to work myself into another frenzy quite yet. I'm finally feeling a little relaxed. Or maybe the word is *safe*. Either way, it occurs to me that the last time I felt this way was the last time I was in this limo with Michael. Does that mean something in this damn puzzle? What part does Michael play?

"I did it again, didn't I?" I say. "I interrupted one of your business dinners."

"Don't worry about it." Michael takes a peek at his platinum Rolex. "As long as I return in time to pick up the check, no one will care."

"Do you really have to go back to the restaurant?" I ask as I take his hand.

"I'm afraid so. Besides, what *you* have to do is get some rest."

He couldn't be more right. My body's officially running on fumes. Except I don't want him to leave me. Couldn't we just drive around in his limo for the rest of our lives?

"Michael?"

"Yes?"

"Will you make love to me?"

He answers with a soft kiss to my lips, barely touching them with his. Just what I need.

Slowly, he undresses me. For a moment my eyes drift from his, and I glance up through the sunroof into the night, the long steel cables of the Brooklyn Bridge hovering above. They're lit with a dreamy yellow hue that reminds me of a vintage photograph, something beautiful and lasting.

Timeless.

Chapter 71

IT'S SO HARD saying good-bye to Michael as we pull up to my building, I almost break into tears. It's even harder to be alone again in my apartment. It feels like forever since it's been home sweet home for me.

The second I get inside my door and lock it, *lock myself in,* the phone starts to ring. I don't want to answer, but maybe it's Michael. He's had second thoughts and he's coming over. *Please, let that be it.*

I pick up on the fifth ring, and it's an operator. "I have a collect call from Kristin Burns." I want to throw down the receiver, but I think about it and I accept the call.

I hear my own voice. "Help me. Please help me. Somebody make it stop!"

Now I throw down the receiver. MAKE WHAT STOP? WHAT IN THE NAME OF GOD IS HAPPENING? HOW CAN I GET A PHONE CALL FROM MYSELF?

The nasty bump on my forehead is definitely real and already ripening to a deep purplish bruise. It's well beyond any cover-up stick, so I fiddle with a new hairstyle—bangs down.

Then I throw on a T-shirt and sweats and crawl into bed. I should be asleep before my head, bump and all, hits the pillow.

So why am I still awake?

Five minutes, ten minutes, a half hour passes, and all I can do is toss and turn. The past few days play over and over in my head, an endless loop of fear and confusion. All the stress that seemed to melt away in Michael's arms begins to seep—then gush—back in.

There's only one thing I can think to do.

I jump up and grab my camera. I can almost hear the voice of Dr. Curley playing his little fill-in-the-blank game with me. *When I'm under stress I like to . . .*

I close the door to my darkroom and start to develop the shot I snapped at the hospital. I don't rush, since there's little doubt as to what I'll see. Dr. Curley wasn't standing there alone; I know I didn't imagine it. And that goes for everything else too.

Now, if I could just figure out what it all means, or at least how it could be happening.

I hold up the picture. There was a time I couldn't look at the face of Dr. Floyd Magnumsen without breaking into tears.

His hands were so cold. He always wore gloves during my checkups, except for that one time. *Why is he locking the door?* I thought. And then I understood: because he didn't want anyone to know that he was a monster.

I felt so ashamed and confused afterward. And then, when no one believed me, I wanted to die.

Dr. Magnumsen wasn't only a respected pediatrician, he was a war hero . . . and I was a twelve-year-old girl with an "active" imagination. Even my parents suspected

I was making the whole thing up. "Are you sure you're not just trying to get attention, Kristin?" my mother asked me. "Are you sure this really happened?"

But then someone else came forward. A sophomore at Concord High School. Dr. Magnumsen had told her he needed to feel for bumps "down there," and that it was okay if it felt good. She'd kept it a secret for over four years.

But when she read about me in the paper and heard the talk on Main Street, the proverbial scarlet *L* for "Liar" being plastered on my faded overalls, she could no longer stay silent. She told what Magnumsen had done to her.

I wasn't alone. *I was telling the truth.*

Two days later, the girl's father stormed into Magnumsen's office and aimed a shotgun at his face. It was a closed-casket funeral, said the newspaper stories.

But here Floyd Magnumsen is now, in my hands, back from the dead. There's not a scratch on him. It's as if I took this picture fifteen years ago.

I pin it up on the wall and add the shots I took to show Javier. I take a step back and study it, knowing this has to be a key to everything that's happening.

But what could Dr. Magnumsen possibly have to do with my father? Or Penley and Michael?

And what do they all have to do with the Fálcon Hotel?

I lean in for a closer look at the gurneys lined up on the sidewalk. Four body bags right in a row. *Who are those people? How did they die?*

Reaching out, I run my fingers across the pictures. As my hand approaches the weirdest of them all — the one of Michael on the floor *that I never took* — it stops.

I hear something. I'm sure of it.

There's a noise outside the darkroom.

Footsteps.

Someone's inside my apartment!

I stop everything—every movement, every muscle. I'm not breathing. I'm not even blinking.

Just listening for another sound.

Only it's gone. I no longer hear anything. My exhausted mind is playing tricks, and here's another reminder that I should be in my bedroom, not my darkroom.

Seriously, call it a night, Kris!

Stifling a yawn, I'm about to head out of the darkroom.

Shit! Shit! Shit!

I hear the footsteps again.

They're right outside the door.

They're not in my head.

And unfortunately, that's not exactly good news.

Chapter 72

I GRAB THE STEEL tripod stashed in the corner of the darkroom. If there's danger waiting for me on the other side of the door, I'm at least going down swinging.

In the sliver of space beneath the door, I can see the shadow of feet—*big feet*—creeping near. I grip the tripod tighter with both hands and pull it back over my shoulder. *Batter up.* Whoever's out there is going to get hurt. I'm in the mood for it.

"Ms. Burns, are you in there?"

I recognize the voice.

I open the door and I'm staring at Detective Frank Delmonico. "How did you get in here?"

"I walked," he answers sardonically. There's not even the hint of an apology from him. "You think maybe I flew in an open window?"

The cocky line works. I'm speechless.

"Your door was open," he says. "I knocked, and I guess you didn't hear me, huh? Now, if you're done with your third degree, it's my turn to ask a few questions."

Delmonico removes the same pen and tattered notepad from inside the same dark gray suit. I smell his aftershave, or whatever it is, and tobacco. Even more than before, the detective gives me the creeps.

This is happening too fast — and too *late* — I think. It's near midnight. *What is this guy doing in my apartment?*

"I told you I'd answer any questions, but does it have to be now?" I ask.

"Yes."

"Why?"

"Because I don't think you've been leveling with me," he says. "And I've got a problem with that."

In light of his tone, that's the understatement of the year.

Be careful, Kris. "All right, how can I help you? I don't know anything about those murders," I blurt out.

"The morning I first saw you outside the Fálcon Hotel, why were you taking so many pictures?" he asks, basically ignoring what I just said to him.

"I'm into photography."

"Is it your profession?"

"Hopefully, one day. I'm up for an important gallery showing. I have an agent. You could talk to her if you want. Maybe *tomorrow.*"

He peers over my shoulder. "Is that your darkroom?"

"Yes."

"Mind if I take a look?" Delmonico says, and he takes a step forward.

I shift my feet to block the way. "Actually, I do."

He smirks. "Are you hiding something from me?

Maybe the pictures you took at the hotel? Or is it something else you don't want me to see?"

"No. My photographs are personal, that's all."

"Duly noted," he says.

Then Delmonico pushes past me.

Right into my darkroom.

Chapter 73

"HEY, WHAT ARE YOU DOING? How dare you!"

Delmonico stops in the middle of my darkroom, staring left and right. My pictures are everywhere. They're like wallpaper. He seems either impressed or overwhelmed by what he sees. "My, my, my," he mutters. "Such a busy, busy girl."

"I didn't give you permission to be in here!" I snap.

He turns to me, his dark eyes boring into my head. "If you'd like, I can come back with a search warrant and turn this entire apartment upside down. Do you want that? Or I could forget about the search warrant and toss your place anyway. You know that good cop–bad cop routine? I'm the *bad* cop, Kristin."

"You're saying I'm a murder suspect?"

"What I'm saying is that you're not cooperating with a murder investigation."

"You can't be serious."

He takes a step toward me. He's nearly twice my size. "In case you conveniently forgot, Ms. Burns, people died that morning. Four of them."

"I know that. I was there."

"And you were acting rather strange, as I recall."

"I was upset." *I still am, buster!*

"Yet you said you didn't know any of them."

"I was upset. I told you that. They were sitting out there on the sidewalk, *dead*."

"But you thought one of them was still alive. That's what you told me, anyway."

"No, what I thought was . . . I mean, yes, but I didn't actually . . . uh . . ."

The more I hesitate, the harder the detective looks at me. I know I'm not making total sense. Worse, I'm digging a deep hole for myself.

"Which is it?" he asks. "Did you or did you not see a dead person come back to life?"

"This is ridiculous. You know I had nothing to do with those murders."

"You're just an innocent bystander, right?"

"Yes."

He laughs in my face. "Is that really what you think you are? Innocent? So virtuous that I have some nerve even talking to you?"

"I don't know what you're implying, but I don't like it. I'm done answering your questions. You can leave."

Delmonico nods, tucking his notepad and pen back into his pocket.

Thank God! He's going.

No.

He's just freeing up his hands.

In a blur, he grabs my shoulders, slamming me against the wall. I hit hard, and pictures go flying, the pain shooting up my spine. I can't believe he just did that.

"Listen to me! Listen to the bad cop!" he says, breathing fire. "You're not done with anything until I say you are. You're wondering whether you're a murder suspect? *Yes,* you're a murder suspect, Miss Burns. For starters."

I can't talk, I'm terrified.

"You really think you're hot shit, don't you? A real *independent* woman," he says. "Well, guess what? It's only a matter of time before I take you down. Because you are involved with those four murders. That much I know."

I open my mouth, fighting first for air, then words. "You're . . . hurting . . . me," I manage.

He shakes his head. "You don't know the meaning of hurt. But you will."

The back of one of his hands slowly drifts down from my neck and across my chest.

This is really happening.

What's he going to do now? Take me in? Arrest me for murders I didn't commit?

His hand stops just above my breast. It's right over my heart, which is beating wildly.

"Do you feel that?" he says. He leans in, his eyes mere inches from mine. He doesn't blink, not once. "When you think of me, you remember that fear."

He pulls back, letting go of me. I start trembling as he walks to the door and turns around.

"I know where you live, Miss Burns," he says. "And I know what you did at the Fálcon Hotel. *Both* times you were there."

Chapter 74

IF THERE IS SUCH A THING as a very bad, very good thing, then that's what I do the next day.

Penley is going to be gone all day at some fancy-schmancy kitchen tour out in South Hampton—so she says, anyway—so instead of taking the kids to school, I call there to say they have the flu, and then we play hooky.

I really feel that Dakota and Sean need this. Especially Dakota. And so do I.

First things first, we have a total pig-out breakfast at Sarabeth's, our favorite restaurant in all of New York. Blueberry and chocolate-chip pancakes, with loads of syrup, for everybody. Then we head off to Central Park with only one purpose in mind: to get absolutely filthy dirty, to be real kids for a change, to have a blast.

For three hours, we run and jump and scream our brains out, play tag, play catch, play keep-away, and I don't have a single crazy thought, don't smell anything bad, don't even see any dead people.

We end up at a little concrete playground with swings

and slides, and Dakota and Sean are grimy dirty — which
I love, and they love too. In fact, I've never seen such big
smiles on either of their faces.

Of course, I have to take photographs of the kids.
Dozens and dozens of beautiful shots. So cute, so
picture-perfect.

And then — disaster strikes!

Sean catches his bright red Keds sneaker on the lad-
der at the top of the slide, and he literally goes head over
heels. I watch and I can't believe what I'm seeing as he
tumbles way too fast, then hits the pavement with his
face. I swear to God, with his forehead.

Ten minutes later, we're at the emergency room at
Lenox Hill, and amazingly, miraculously, Sean is totally
okay and doesn't even need a stitch. He even gets a lol-
lipop, and so does Dakota.

It's quiet in the cab from Lenox Hill going home, and
then Dakota leans into me and puts her head on my shoulder. I wish I could take a picture of the two of us.

"It's all right, Miss Kristin. It's all right," she says.
"We won't tell."

"Promise," says Sean. "We won't tell. We love you,
Miss Kristin."

And I love these kids so much.

I just love Dakota and Sean to death. Who wouldn't?

I also feel guilty, and I don't know how to get away
from that. Not about playing hooky for one stupid day,
which was great — but about everything else.

And I mean *everything* else.

Chapter 75

HELL, I SHOULD JUST TOSS my alarm clock out the window. What's that joke Sean likes to tell? About seeing time fly?

Really, what's the point of an alarm clock when I've got this dreaded dream to wake me every morning? I get the feeling it's going to be with me for an awfully long time. Like forever.

Same for all the other bizarre stuff filling my days. And all I can do is wonder, *Can I really handle this?*

Can I get on with my life, such as it is?

Damn it, I'm going to try. With a little help from my friends.

Beth and Connie conference call me on my cell phone minutes after I drop off Dakota and Sean at school. They want to take me to lunch and won't take no for an answer.

Of course, what they really want to do is see if I'm okay or completely mashed potatoes. The social worker in Connie undoubtedly has her hyperconcerned after my surprise sleepover-cum-meltdown at her apartment. Naturally, Beth heard all about it.

Imagine if I tell them everything that's occurred since.
Only that's not going to happen.

That monster Delmonico has me scared silent. About everything. I can still feel his grip on my neck, the look in his eyes.

Anyway, it's with an "all's well" attitude that I walk into the Comfort Diner—how fitting—on 45th Street between Second and Third. Connie and Beth are already seated at a table by the window, and I make sure to greet them with a healthy smile.

Unfortunately, the rest of my body didn't get the memo.

"You look like shit, Kris," says Beth almost immediately.

Connie rolls her eyes while I enjoy a much-needed laugh. There's blunt, and then there's Beth. No wonder she has such a hard time finding acting work. She once told Martin Scorsese that he needed to "trim those caterpillars" above his eyes.

"You do look a bit tired, Kristin," says Connie, trying to be a little more diplomatic and gentle. "Have you been getting enough sleep?"

"I certainly got plenty at your place the other night," I say.

"Until you woke up screaming like my apartment was in a wing at Bellevue," she points out.

As if I need to be reminded.

"Have you been to see a doctor?" asks Beth. "Maybe you've got a virus."

"And what about seeing your psychiatrist again?" says Connie in tow. "Have you given that any more thought?"

Call me crazy, but I think I'm done with psychiatrists.
I look at the two of them, their faces full of genuine

concern. "Listen, I know you guys are trying to help and I appreciate it, I really do. But right now, the best thing for me is to have a fun lunch with my girlfriends. Can we do that? You think?"

They both nod, getting the point. I need to be *distracted,* not prodded. So they dig deep into their daily lives and share the best stories they can think of.

Connie kicks things off by telling us about the guy from her office who got caught making photocopies of his penis. I don't believe her, but she swears it's true.

"I bet he was using the enlarge button," quips Beth.

We laugh and order, and by the time our food arrives, the conversation has made its way around to my job and the wonderful Penley.

"Let me guess," says Beth. "While we're stuffing our faces, the Pencil's at the gym, burning off her last remaining calorie."

"She definitely is a gym rat," I say. "Though right now she's out in Greenwich for some charity lunch."

"You know, we really should meet her," says Connie.

Beth raises a brow. "Why on earth would we want to do *that?*"

"Yeah, you're probably right. What do you think, Kris?"

"I think she's better left to your imagination," I say with a chuckle. God, *that* feels good.

Connie smiles and digs back into her chef's salad. I'm reaching for my iced tea when Beth starts to giggle. She's looking out the window.

"Check out that serious PDA going on across the street," she says, pointing.

Connie and I follow her finger to see a man and

woman engaged in a serious lip-lock right under a "Don't Walk" sign. There's not an inch of daylight between them as their "public display of affection" seems to last forever. Eventually, the woman pulls back, playfully pushing the man while glancing about as though to see if anyone's watching.

"Omigod!" I sputter.

Connie and Beth turn to me in unison. "What is it?" asks Connie.

"That's Penley!"

"Are you serious, Kris? You're joking, right? Tell me you're joking."

"I thought you said she was out in Greenwich," says Beth.

"I know. That's what she told me."

The three of us look back out the window. The man is whispering something in Penley's ear. Sweet nothings, it appears.

"Wow," says Beth. "You never mentioned how good-looking her husband is."

"You're right," I say. "Only that's not her husband."

Chapter 76

I JUMP UP FROM MY CHAIR, jolting the table and nearly knocking over my iced tea. I sprint for the door with a hurried "good-bye" to my friends.

"Kris, wait!" I hear Connie call.

But I don't. I can't. This could be important, a key to unraveling everything.

Spilling out of the restaurant, I immediately look across the street. The "Don't Walk" sign now reads "Walk." And Penley's gone.

So is Stephen. Tall, dark, and handsome Stephen. Her lover, from the look of it.

Quickly glancing around, I spot the couple farther down the sidewalk. Before I know it, I'm following them.

I can't believe this. The plot, as they say, is thickening.

Not only is Penley having an affair, the guy is someone she set me up with as a blind date!

But for all my disbelief, there's something else.

Relief.

I've been dragging a full measure of guilt like a

heavy suitcase since the first day Michael—"a married man"—and I got together.

But now, seeing Penley cheating on him, suddenly I don't feel so bad.

Yeah, I know, two wrongs don't exactly make a right. *It simply makes it a little easier.*

I continue to follow Stephen and Penley. They're not arm in arm or holding hands, and to the passerby they could just as easily be friends as lovers.

That is, until they reach another "Don't Walk" sign. It's as if something comes over them, or, more specifically, over Stephen. As they stand waiting at the corner, he can't take his hands—or lips—off her.

Penley doesn't stop him, but I can tell she's aware they're out in public. She has a lot of friends in the city, and though they're mixed in with about eight million strangers, one can't be too careful. There's no telling when someone she knows might see her.

Like me.

The "Walk" sign flashes, and the make-out session gives way to their continuing stroll. I fall right in step while confronting my next emotion. *Fear.*

There's no way Penley and Stephen only started seeing each other in the past couple of days, and that can mean only one thing.

She knows.

Something, at least. If Penley doesn't know for sure about Michael and me, she at least suspects. What else could explain Stephen's dinner talk about being involved with someone married? Was he trying to help her get a confession from me or was it all about screwing with my mind?

Either way, Penley's "setting me up" with Stephen was truly a setup! And I didn't see it.

This changes everything.

The two of them come to a stop at the next corner, and Stephen picks up where he left off with more tonsil hockey and some pretty serious groping. Penley's going at it now too. They *really* ought to get a room.

I stand on the sidewalk a half block behind them and miles away from being able to collect all my thoughts and emotions about this new development. There's so much to think about; there are so many angles to consider.

That's when I realize what I should be doing.

Don't think, just shoot.

I reach for my camera. If I'm quick enough, I'll get them tongue kissing before the light changes.

Only I don't feel anything where I'm reaching.

No camera. No shoulder bag. I forgot to grab it when I bolted out of the Comfort Diner.

Shit fire and save matches! I think.

And I remember who used to say that—*my dead father.*

Chapter 77

"WHAT?" SAYS MICHAEL.

I start to repeat myself, but he heard me the first time. He just can't believe it. Or is it *me* he can't believe?

We're standing before floor-to-ceiling windows in the living room of the Wall Street apartment his company provides for out-of-town VIPs. Apparently there are a lot of them, because we've only been able to meet here a few times. Those were romantic interludes, however, and something tells me there'll be a lot less sex tonight.

"Are you sure it was Penley?" Michael asks. "This isn't just a fantasy you're having?"

"I'm positive. I saw it with my own eyes."

I'm trying to put myself in his shoes. Less than forty-eight hours ago he was rescuing me from a Brooklyn hospital before they could check me into a padded room.

Now this bombshell.

Maybe I'd be a little skeptical too. Especially when I tell Michael that I didn't have my camera with me. He knows I practically sleep with it.

So with no pictures—*no proof*—all I've got is my word and his trust in me.

"And you're sure it was the same guy she set you up with?" he asks.

I nod. "Yes, it was that 'cute guy,' Stephen."

"That would mean . . ."

"Exactly," I say.

"But how could she know? We've been careful."

I shoot him a dubious look. "I distinctly recall the Maytag club, among other things."

"Still, I'd *know* if she knew. Penley would be trying to kill me, not playing games." He begins to pace, thinking out loud. His neck and face are getting very red. "She sent this guy out to dinner with you on a reconnaissance mission? I mean, the woman has balls, but we're talking King Kong cojones here."

"It doesn't seem so crazy if she only *suspected* we were involved."

"Trust me," he says. "What you're telling me is crazy no matter how you slice it."

The word seems to hang in the air—right above my head. *Crazy.* Does he think that's what I am? Also, he's starting to get very pissed. Maybe even at me. *I do not need one of your meltdowns here, Michael.*

"You don't believe me, do you?" I say.

Michael abruptly stops pacing. He comes over and takes me in his arms. "Of course I believe you," he says. He tacks on a loving squeeze lest there be any doubt.

But there is doubt. I can hear it in his voice. I see it in his eyes. He's not really sure what to think.

Of all the ways I thought he might react to the news, uncertainty wasn't in the mix. I could understand his anger, and even resentment. I could tolerate a twinge of jealousy. No man likes to share a woman, regardless of whether he loves her.

Nonetheless, when the emotional dust settled, what I hoped for from Michael was that he'd see this the same way I now do—as an opportunity. No longer the only adulterer in his marriage, he won't have to worry about being raked over the coals in a divorce settlement. Once and for all, he can do what I've always wanted him to do.

Dump Penley.

"So now what?" I ask.

"I want to sleep on it," he says. He stares at me for a moment. "You're absolutely sure it was her, though, right, Kris? You're certain."

"Yes," I answer. "I saw them."

I'm sure of it.

At least I think I am.

Chapter 78

ALL NIGHT I TOSS and turn, thinking about Penley and Stephen, and whether Michael believes me. Or for that matter whether I believe me.

The only silver lining is that I'm spared again from the dream when morning arrives. If only I could figure out how to live the rest of my life without sleep, I'd be all set.

When I arrive for work, Penley does a double take. "You forgot what day it is, didn't you?" she says.

I smack my forehead. "You're right, I did."

Once every two weeks, Penley steps in for me and walks Dakota and Sean to school. I get the morning off.

Michael calls it her "guilt trip," but I don't think guilt has anything to do with it. If it did, it would mean she's aware of what a bad mother she is. And about *that* she's definitely clueless. Rather, in her oh-so-twisted mind, Penley probably sees subbing for me as a required sacrifice. Community service, with her children.

"Well, since you're here," says Penley, "the chaise cushions for the patio need to be brought out for the summer. Make sure you thoroughly clean the furniture first, okay?"

"No problem," I say.

"And the cushions, of course."

"Sure thing."

She folds her arms across her Chanel gym outfit, which cost more than a month of my salary. "After I drop off the kids, I'm going for a workout. I should be home by lunch, though."

"That reminds me," I say, "how was your charity luncheon out in Greenwich yesterday?"

I watch her carefully, hoping Penley flinches or blinks or stammers — something that gives her away.

Instead, she's seamless. "Oh, you know how those things are. You've been to one, you've been to them all."

I bet.

Penley heads for her bedroom to continue getting ready, and I check on Dakota and Sean in the kitchen, where they're finishing up their breakfast. Their mother microwaves a mean bowl of instant oatmeal.

"Hi, Miss Kristin!" they giddily say in unison. They're surprised to see me. And happy!

"What are you *doing* here?" asks Sean.

"Yeah, I thought it was Mommy's day to take us to school," says Dakota.

"It is, honey. Silly me, I forgot."

"But you never forget," she says.

"Never *ever*," adds Sean.

I look at them both and smile. Kids are so smart.

They're right. I *didn't* forget.

Not by a long shot.

With a zoom lens.

Chapter 79

TEN MINUTES LATER, I follow Penley and the kids to school, hopefully at a safe distance. If any of them spots me, I'm dead. Let me change that to *toast*.

For maybe the tenth time I check to see that my camera is tucked safely in my shoulder bag and that the bag is actually by my side.

Up ahead, Penley, Dakota, and Sean are just past halfway to Preston Academy. It truly is a perfect opportunity for a mother to spend some quality time with her kids. Too bad Penley's gabbing away on her cell phone, paying no attention whatsoever to Sean and Dakota.

Not that I mind. It keeps her distracted. It keeps her from looking over her shoulder.

With each step in their shadows, I can't help thinking how strange this feels, almost like an out-of-body experience. Most every morning, that's me up there with Dakota and Sean.

To see someone else in my place makes me realize even more how important those kids are to me. I always want to be there for them. I also know it would be selfish and wrong of me to want this if Penley was any kind of a decent mom.

We cover another block heading south and, yet again, I check to make sure I've got my camera.

Minutes later, I duck into a phone kiosk and watch Penley in front of the school's gates as she practically shoos Dakota and Sean away. Amazingly, she's *still* on her cell.

Is she talking to Stephen?

Is he meeting her at the gym?

"Excuse me, are you using that phone?" I hear.

The man's voice startles me. *Does it sound familiar? Actually, yes.*

I turn around to see a guy in baggy jeans and a Gap T-shirt. *Damn it, I know him!* I haven't seen this guy since we were in high school together. I have no idea what happened to him after school, but here he is, wandering into my nightmare.

I point at the phone. "I don't think anyone's using it," I say. "You're Harvey, right? From Concord?"

He stares at the frayed wire jutting from the receiver like a rat's tail. "There's a call coming for you, Kristin," he says. Matter-of-fact, just like that.

Then the phone rings, and I literally jump. But I sure don't answer it.

"Yeah. I'm Harvey," he says, then he shuffles off.

"And let me guess," I say to him. "You're dead, right?" But Harvey doesn't bother to answer.

I immediately turn back to Penley standing in front of the school. Only she's not there. Oh, great.

My head turns like one of those automatic sprinklers. Not until my second three sixty do I spot her humping down Madison. Her walk gives her away. "I'm better than you," it says with each stride. "So get out of my way!"

I hurry across the street, falling in behind her again. Now that the kids are gone, she's off the phone. I'm shielded by the crowded sidewalk—the morning rush hour traffic—but I'm careful not to get too close.

We head south a few more blocks, and I try to remember what gym she belongs to. Is it Reebok? Equinox? Did she ever even tell me?

Anyway, I'll find out soon enough. If I know Penley, it can't be too much farther. Otherwise, she would've cabbed it, for sure.

My eyes remain trained on her while my mind looks ahead. *One kiss,* that's all I need. A suggestive embrace would do the job, but a kiss, that would be the money shot.

That's assuming Stephen's even there.

She told me the gym is where they met. Then again, she also said he and I would make a nice couple. *Ha!*

Maybe this is nothing more than a wild goose chase and maybe it isn't. I don't care. I'm determined to get the proof I need—that Michael needs—if it's there to get.

Then why am I starting to feel so uneasy about this?

There's a hollow forming in my stomach, and with each step it grows. It's not nerves or nausea, it's something different. And this isn't the first time I've felt it.

Streets, time, everything seems a blur to me. I'm so pre-occupied with the feeling, I almost miss Penley's arrival at her gym.

I focus my eyes and watch her walk in. At that exact

moment, the feeling takes over, consuming me. I know what it is. *Dread.*

And I know when I felt it last too.

Here.

Right outside Penley's "gym."

Otherwise known as the Fálcon Hotel.

Chapter 80

I WANT TO RUN, but I can't decide which way to go.

I'm desperate to get the hell out of here, and yet I absolutely have to keep following Penley and see where this is going. I take a step forward, then back. I'm a human yo-yo.

Finally, I run.

To the hotel.

I push back the fear—the dread—and sprint up the front steps beneath the Fálcon's red awning, slowing down only as I enter the lobby. *Which I remember—from my time here after I moved from Boston. Block it out, Kris. Not relevant now.*

Here comes the first tricky part—seeing which room Penley's heading to while still not being seen.

Where is she?

Nowhere. I scan the swank lobby with its minimalist decor. They've redecorated, I see. The furniture is all black, as is most of the clothing. It's like a Prada convention. There are thin people everywhere, but not one of them is Penley.

I rush to the two elevators on the wall to the left of reception. The first is open and waiting, the second heading upward. A digital panel on the wall tells me where. I watch and wait until it stops on the fourth floor.

Off I go, taking the empty elevator. When the doors open, I peek out, hoping to see Penley from behind, moving toward a room.

Instead, the hallway's empty. I feel like one of those characters in a scary movie, with the audience shouting, *"Get out of there, Kristin. Run! Get away!"*

I won't do that. I worry that I've missed Penley or that she's not even on this floor.

Then comes a woman's laugh from a few rooms down. *Or is it a cackle?* Either way, I know it instantly. It's the Pencil.

I get close and listen, my ear maybe an inch from the door. When they're not laughing, they're talking, and though I can't quite make out the conversation, I recognize the other voice in the room. It's him.

Stephen.

I listen for a minute to their frolicking. They almost sound like kids in there, albeit very naughty ones. Is this really the woman who has me alphabetize her cans of soup?

I feel for my camera again. No problem this time — it's there. At the ready.

I spot the door to the stairwell at the end of the hallway. There's a small cut-out window at eye level. Looks like a perfect place to set up shop.

I figure if Penley and Stephen arrive separately, they probably leave separately. Not that it really makes a difference. Solo shots of them slinking out of the same hotel room will more than do the trick. Michael will be able to fill in the blanks.

I back away from the door, the mix of their giggling and God-knows-what now like nails on a blackboard to me. If I'm going to commit to a stakeout, I can only hope that Stephen isn't into tantric sex, like Sting. *I'll be waiting forever!*

I start walking toward the stairwell. Halfway there, I stop as if I've hit a wall. The feeling of dread rushes over me again as I turn and face a room on the opposite side of the hallway. I feel dizzy; I'm shivering.

All because of what I hear.

Chapter 81

IT'S THE MUSIC!

This time it's not between my ears, it's behind the door. The same song that accompanies the dream—*about this hotel!*—is coming from inside this other room. It must be on the radio. How convenient. Or how sadistic of someone. But who?

I lean in and listen, my ears straining. It's faint, and I still can't make out the damn lyrics. The name of the song remains stuck on the tip of my tongue.

Not for long, though.

I knock softly on the door. *I hate to bother you, folks, but it's time to play Name That Tune!*

No one answers.

So I knock a little louder.

C'mon, answer already!

Are you in the shower?

Asleep? With the radio on? I guess it could happen.

I drop to my knees, peering in at what little I can see beneath the door. *It's definitely dark in there.*

This is so frustrating! Whatever it takes, I *need* to get into that room right now.

I stand and begin banging furiously, my fist bruising right before my eyes. If no one's in there, I'll knock down the damn door myself!

I hear a lock snapping open.

Behind me!

It's Penley and Stephen's room.

RUN!

I sprint for all I'm worth toward the stairwell. From behind me, I can hear the door opening and Stephen's voice echoing in the hallway.

"I don't know; I'll check," he's saying to Penley. "I heard it too. I'm *checking.*"

Stupid, stupid, stupid! I was too loud!

I reach the stairwell entrance, frantically pushing through the door. Did he see me? Would he recognize me from behind? Or from the *front,* for that matter?

I'm about to race down the stairs when my gut steers me in the opposite direction. *Up! Go up!*

Dashing up the steps, I reach the landing halfway to the next floor and throw myself against the cold concrete wall, out of view, I hope. I hold my breath, listening for Stephen.

Sure enough, he was right behind me. He's running *down* the stairs. My gut was right.

I tiptoe to the railing and steal a quick glance. A couple of flights below, I can see the top of Stephen's head. Also on display are his bare shoulders. He's wearing nothing but a towel.

He continues downward, probably thinking I'm headed for the lobby.

That's when I hear it. The voice I love to hate.

"Honey?" Penley calls out. "Where are you?"

On a dime, he stops. Penley must have him wrapped around her bony little finger.

"I'm down here," he calls back.

"Who was making the noise in the hall?" she asks.

"That's what I'm trying to find out."

"Oh, I see. So you'd rather run around the hotel half naked than have sex with me? Okay. Fine."

It's classic Penley. And before you can say "horndog," Stephen's racing back up the stairs to her.

It's a miracle, all right.

Praise the Pencil!

Chapter 82

"YOU'RE *WHERE?*" he asks.

"Outside the Fálcon Hotel," I answer. "Where you need to be right away. Please come. . . . Yes, I want you to drop everything."

I quickly explain why.

"I'll be right there," Michael tells me. "Don't move."

"Don't worry, I won't."

I don't. I remain perched on a stool behind the window of a Starbucks across the street. There's a perfect view of the Fálcon's entrance, the red awning eclipsed only by the occasional bus or delivery truck passing by. After Stephen chased me into that stairwell, I wasn't exactly in the mood to stick around inside. Plus, there's the matter of my history with the hotel. Poor little Kristin's first days in New York. A horror story in itself. But definitely one for another time.

Anyway, a picture might be worth a thousand words, but having Michael see Penley's affair in the flesh — *as it were* — speaks for itself.

Now he has to get here before they leave. Which

means I change my mind about one thing: I hope Stephen *does* have sex like Sting . . . on one of his best days too.

Twenty minutes later, Michael storms through the door of Starbucks. All at once, the loitering latte drinkers glance up from their laptops.

"What the hell are you looking at?" says Michael's expression. "Go back to writing your stupid spec screenplays that will never get made!"

He spots me and hurries over. "They still in there?" he asks, nodding at the hotel.

"Yes, thankfully," I answer.

He frowns, and I get it immediately. *Thankfully* really isn't the right word. As much as he wants to catch Penley red-handed, I have to remember this isn't something he relishes.

In fact, he seems completely on edge and on the verge of going over the top, which is something I don't want to experience.

That look of doubting me, of thinking that I'm "Crazy Kristin," is entirely gone from his eyes, though. He knows I'm not mistaken or making it up. This is *real*.

He asks me to tell him everything again, from my first steps following Penley to when I called his office. "Give me every detail, Kris," he says. And I do. Right down to their room number.

Of course, there is one thing I leave out, and that's the other room and the music. *Was there really no one in there? Was there even music playing?*

Michael pulls back a sleeve to reveal his Rolex. "How long has it been?"

"About an hour," I say, watching him tap his loafer

impatiently. "Just so you know, they'll probably come out separately. That's how they arrived."

He bristles. "She's walking out of a *hotel,* for Christ's sake. At eleven in the morning. Alone or not, what more do I need to see?"

He sees it anyway, the whole sloppy enchilada.

To my utter disbelief, Penley and Stephen emerge together seconds later. How brazen. How stupid. How very Penley.

And how enraged Michael becomes.

I'm watching him watch them, his face reddening, his nostrils flaring. Maybe a picture *would've* been better. I'm afraid he might explode right here in the coffee shop.

Then it gets even worse.

Penley and Stephen engage in one hot and heavy, no doubt about it kiss. It's the money shot, and while I no longer need to capture it on film, I do anyway. The photographer's instinct takes over. Don't think, just shoot.

As for Michael, it's as if he's watching a spectacular car wreck. He can't turn away from the Kiss. I don't really blame him. It is compelling stuff, in a sick sort of way.

"Unfuckingbelievable," he mutters under his breath. "Un-*fucking*-believable."

I lower my camera and look at him. It's his voice. I've never heard it like this before. The tone, the register — it's beyond anger. It's beyond anything.

"Are you okay?" I ask. "Michael? I'm sorry you had to see this."

"I could kill the bitch" is his answer.

Chapter 83

MY MIND IS SPINNING a little, but Michael's seems completely focused, locked in. For the first time I can see how he is at his job. "Where does she think you are right now?" he asks.

I barely hear him. "Huh?"

"*Penley*—does she think you're at the apartment?"

I nod, and he immediately whips out his cell phone.

"What are you doing?" I ask.

"Would you ever disappear from work this long without leaving a note?"

He's right. I didn't think that far ahead. "No," I say. "In fact, I'm supposed to be getting the patio cleaned up for summer."

Michael hits his speed dial. "So we need to buy you some time," he says.

The next moment borders on surreal. So what's new? I watch across the street as Penley breaks her lip-lock with Stephen and reaches into her purse. She checks her cell phone and immediately looks uneasily at Stephen, raising a finger to her mouth. *Shhh.*

She answers the phone, and I see her lips moving. This is weird but also exciting.

"Hi, honey, how are you?" says Michael, standing about a foot away from me. "You still at the gym?"

His voice is completely normal, even chipper, not a hint of stress.

This is so bizarre, I'm thinking. Of course, this is also so Michael, the same guy who threw his arm around my shoulder and introduced me to everyone at his business dinner. One cool cucumber.

I've got my eyes trained on Penley as my ears pick up her voice through Michael's phone. It's sort of like watching a foreign movie with subtitles.

"I'm leaving the gym now," I hear her answer. "What do you want? I'm kind of busy at the moment."

"You must be *exhausted,*" says Michael. He shoots me a grin. She's not the only one with King Kong balls.

I strain to hear what Penley says next, something about why Michael is on his cell and not in his office.

"Oh, I'm just out grabbing a cup of coffee," he replies. "You know how I hate the crap they brew at the office; it's weak as shit. Actually, that's why I'm calling. I need a favor."

Penley tells him to hold on for a second.

Michael and I watch through the window as she puts her hand over the phone and says something to Stephen, who appears to be losing his patience. *Poor guy.* Clearly she's explaining that she can't ditch Michael's call easily. A few seconds later, a frustrated Stephen marches back into the hotel.

What, does he live there?

Penley gets back on. "So what's the favor?"

"Is everything okay?" asks Michael.

"Yeah. For a second I thought I left my keys at the gym. I found them, though."

Pretty clever, Penley.

"So, about that favor," says Michael. "We've got a client coming in from Tokyo tomorrow morning, and someone told me that store in Midtown, Takashimaya, sells this amazing Japanese coffee. I was wondering if you could pick some up for me on your way home."

Penley sighs so annoyingly loud through the phone that a few people sitting nearby turn their heads. They probably can't believe what a bitch she is.

"You can't send your *secretary* to do this?" she whines. "I have to go buy *coffee* for you?"

"Honey, it would take Amanda over an hour to get there and back. I figured you were only a few blocks away. Please, Pen. Could you?"

Another sigh, even louder. "So what's this supposedly *amazing* coffee called?"

"I'm not sure, but I'll recognize the name. Call me on my cell when you get there, okay?"

"Fine."

Penley gives her phone the finger as she flips it closed. All Michael can do is laugh.

"I'm going to miss the little woman," he jokes as Penley disappears from our view.

I smile, but only because I'm glad he can joke at all. I've never seen him as dark as he was a few minutes ago.

I shoot him a look. "Japanese coffee?"

"God is in the details, remember?"

I nod. "So, what now?"

Michael takes my hand. "You love me, don't you?"

"Of course I do."

"And you trust me, right?"

"Yes." *What's this about? Why do I need to trust Michael right now?*

"What you do," he says, "is go back to work, get that patio in order, and pretend that everything's fine and dandy on the home front."

"That's it?"

"For the time being, that's it."

"What about you?"

He doesn't answer. He lets go of my hand and walks toward the door.

"Michael, what are you going to do?"

He glances back, flashes me his best smile. Then he winks. It's *my* wink.

"You'll see."

Chapter 84

GO AFTER HIM! Find out what he's up to. Now, Kristin.

But my feet won't move.

I remain there in the Starbucks window. I watch Michael leave, hop into a cab, ride off. Gone.

"You'll see," he said.

Two little words that paralyze me and start me shaking again. Somehow I know that this is it: where everything has been going from the beginning. But how exactly will it end?

Or do I already know that too?

I look across the street at the Fálcon Hotel, the late-morning sun reflecting off its windows with a fierce glare. I can still picture the scene so clearly—the gurneys being wheeled out, the four body bags lined up on the sidewalk. Cops everywhere. Delmonico. Was the Ponytail there too?

First I dream it. Then I see it. Now it's haunting me every minute of the day.

I know this is all connected; it has to be. But I can't figure it out. Could anybody? I wonder.

Eventually, I move my feet. I rush back to Fifth Avenue and take care of the stupid patio in plenty of time before Penley returns home. When she does, sure enough, she's sporting a shopping bag from Takashimaya with a pound of Japanese coffee inside.

Later, I pick up the kids from school and take them to the Ancient Playground in Central Park, where we've gone dozens of times before. Sean peppers me with one question after another while Dakota rolls her big blue eyes. But we have fun—under the circumstances, anyway.

It's another typical day, all right, everything fine and dandy, just as Michael wanted it.

But for what reason?

"You'll see," he said.

As I head home to my apartment, I get this awful, gnawing feeling that somehow I already have.

Chapter 85

OH, GREAT, JUST WHO I want to see.

My lovely neighbor Mrs. Rosencrantz is standing by the mailboxes as I walk into the lobby of my building. It's almost as if she's there waiting for me.

Turns out, she is.

"Have you gotten your mail yet today?" she asks, her smug tone laced with a small measure of glee.

Actually, I haven't gotten my mail for about a week. I've been a little distracted.

"Why do you care?" I say.

She glares through her oversize bifocals, baiting me by saying nothing. There's obviously something she wants me to see.

I'm tempted to keep walking toward the elevator, not give her the satisfaction, but my curiosity wins out. Maybe I need to solve a mystery, *any* mystery. I unlock my box and remove a pile of catalogues, bills, and other assorted junk mail.

It's right on top.

An envelope from Priority Holdings, the management

company that owns the building. Inside is a one-page letter, single-spaced.

Dear Ms. Burns:
Due to continuing complaints from other tenants
regarding your conduct, we will not be offering you
a rent renewal on your apartment when your cur-
rent lease expires. Under New York State law you
have the right to contest this decision and request an
administrative hearing in accordance with the New
York City Housing Authority.

There's another paragraph about whom to contact, but my attention immediately focuses on whom to blame for this outrage. I don't have to look far.

"This was your doing, wasn't it?"

Mrs. Rosencrantz strikes a priggish pose. "I tend to think you did it to yourself."

"Unbelievable. You really have nothing better to do with your time, huh?" I say, shaking the letter in her face.

"It's not like I didn't warn you this morning."

"This morning?"

"You were terribly rude to me at your door. You have no manners, young woman. None."

"Mrs. Rosencrantz, for your information that wasn't this morning; that was a week ago."

"My *information* is fine, Ms. Burns. I think I know when I knocked on your apartment door."

"Apparently you don't. And in any event, if you think I'm going to let you get away with this, you're sadly mistaken. I'll fight this like you won't believe."

"Go ahead, make all the noise you want. Scream, if you have to. Lord knows you're good at that."

Oh, is she asking for it!

For the first time in my life, I'm tempted to punch an old lady. And what's with her memory? She can't even get her days straight.

But I keep my cool. I summon every last ounce of will-power and walk away. *You've got bigger fish to fry, Kris.*

I move to the elevator and press the up button. As I wait, another letter from the building's management catches my eye. A note, really. It's taped to the wall.

Due to a problem with the furnace, the building was without hot water for a brief period early this morning. We apologize for any inconvenience.

Obviously, the note is from a week ago and they forgot to take it down. *Boy, do I remember that cold shower!*

But as I look closer, there's just one problem.

The note's dated *today*.

Chapter 86

CALM DOWN, I tell myself. *There's a simple explanation.* It happened *again,* that's all. The hot water was out this morning *and* the morning Mrs. Rosencrantz came banging on my door. Two *different* days. As far as what the nasty old bat claims, she's clearly going senile.

I hop on the elevator, my head a jumbled mess. I've never been much of a drinker, but I have a feeling that could change tonight.

Barely inside my apartment, I pour myself a Stoli. A vodka tonic minus the tonic. Then I gulp it like a shot. The only thing I want to feel right now is numb.

I wish Michael could be with me. Better yet, I wish I knew what he was thinking. *Why didn't he want to tell me?* I worry about that temper of his too.

I pour another Stoli and page him while I clench the diamond-and-sapphire bracelet he gave me. I bet he wouldn't mind now if I wore it to work.

A few minutes pass. The waiting is excruciating.

I picture him in a late meeting at Baer Stevens, or on an overseas call, unable to break away. Maybe he's with his lawyer, planning an exit strategy. There's a lot of money at stake in divorcing Penley.

A few minutes turn into a half hour, and the anger begins to kick in. I can't take this. Why isn't Michael calling me back? He has to know we need to talk.

I page him again.

Only now it's not anger driving me, it's fear. *Has he done something? What might he do?*

I hit *67 and dial him at home. I know Penley never gets the phone, but maybe he will.

It rings and rings. *Damn it.*

The answering machine comes on, and I'm about to hang up when I hear "Hello?" I recognize her accent immediately. It's Maria. Only today's not one of the days she cleans. In fact, it's not even "day" anymore; it's night.

"Maria, it's me, Kristin," I say, trying not to sound anxious. "What are you doing there?"

"I'm babysitting," she answers. "Mrs. Turnbull call me last minute to come over."

"Where's Mr. Turnbull?"

"With Mrs. Turnbull. They go out to dinner."

That stops me cold. Dinner? *Together?* "You don't know where they went, do you?"

"No. They give me cell phone numbers in case of emergency. I call them, you want."

"No, no, that's okay."

"When they come home later, I say you call."

"No! Don't—" I catch myself and settle down. "I mean, that's not necessary. I'll talk to Mrs. Turnbull tomorrow."

I thank Maria and hang up, not knowing whether to be relieved or even more worried. Probably the latter. After the way Michael reacted to seeing Penley this morning, the last thing I'd expect would be their having dinner together.

Unless of course there's more to it. As in, *what Michael's not telling me.*

I page Michael again. If he's really having dinner with Penley, why can't he simply excuse himself and return my call?

I start to cry and hate that I do. I can't help myself, though. The more I dwell on this, the harder it gets to take.

I'm about to pour myself another drink when I realize it's not alcohol that I need.

I need my darkroom.

A minute later, under the faint red glow of my safety light, I get busy developing the film I snapped of Penley and Stephen outside the Fálcon. I still can't believe they walked out of there together. Maybe it's true what they say: people having affairs secretly want to get caught.

Whether that's really the case with Penley and Stephen isn't clear.

But soon, as I stare at the first shot of them, I see what is. *No!*

Stephen's image is transparent.

Just like Penley's.

Just like the body bags.

But it still doesn't make sense.

My dream is more than a dream. It's real. It happened. *Past tense.* I know because I was there.

And it's not only me, is it? Someone else knows I was at the Fálcon.

Of course, he's about the last person on Earth I want to see again. Am I so nuts that I'd seek him out?

No, just very, very desperate.

Chapter 87

I DIG THE CARD he gave me out of my shoulder bag, bold black lettering printed on thick white stock. *Detective Frank Delmonico, 19th Precinct, 153 E. 67th Street.*

Just the sight of his name makes me uneasy. The phone number is crossed out and another is written above it in pen. A couple of the digits I can't make out, not that it matters. I have no intention of letting him know I'm coming, of course. I'm banking on the element of surprise. That, and something else.

Only a complete idiot would physically assault me in a building filled with cops.

Taking deep breaths most of the way, I cab it over to the East Side, the precinct mere blocks from the Fálcon. Amid the streetlamps and multiple floodlights, the stone building seems to glow under the night sky. It's actually quite beautiful, albeit in a foreboding kind of way.

In fact, given different circumstances, I'd be reaching for my camera to shoot it. Not now, though.

I've taken enough scary pictures for a while.

As I walk inside, two young policemen are walking

out, deep in conversation. One glances my way, giving
me a quick nod and a smile. I'm about to ask him if
Delmonico is here, when from the corner of my eye I see
what looks like the front desk.

Behind it sits another officer, a hard-nosed type, much
older, bulky, red faced, Irish as Paddy's pig. He's typing
something into a computer as I approach him.

"Help you?" he says without so much as looking up
from the monitor. So far he'd never be able to pick me
out of a lineup.

"Yes," I answer. "I'm here to see Detective Frank
Delmonico."

His stubby fingers practically freeze on the keyboard.
Slowly, he turns to me, his eyes collapsing into a squint.
"Excuse me?"

What's that supposed to mean? "Is Detective Delmonico here or isn't he?"

He shakes his head. "No, he's not here."

"Do you know where he is?"

"Matter of fact, I do. *He's dead.* That's where he is."

I take a wobbly step back. "*What?* I just saw him. He
came to my apartment."

The officer leans forward in his chair.

"When was this?"

"A few days ago."

"I think you're mistaken, Miss—I don't think I caught
the name?"

"No, I'm sure of it. He was at my apartment."

He nods, stifles a chuckle. "Oh, yeah?"

How can he be so cavalier about this? "I'm telling you
the truth. Actually, I talked to him several times in the
past week. He's very thin. Older?"

The officer leans forward even farther, stone-faced. "Now, let me tell *you* the truth," he says slowly. *"Delmonico has been dead for over three years."*

I stand there in stunned silence as the precinct lobby begins to whirl around me. I can feel the blood draining from my head. My knees are starting to go.

"Hey, you okay?"

No, I'm not. I'm absolutely, positively not okay. "Are you sure we're talking about the same guy?" I ask. "Detective Frank Delmonico? Homicide?"

"Yep. Frank Delmonico." He mutters something else under his breath.

"What? I didn't hear that last part."

"It was nothing."

"It was obviously *something*. What was it?"

He glares at me. *Who does this chick think she is?*

But I don't back down. I actually raise my voice. "I want to know what you said!"

The cop shrugs. "Hey, if you insist. I said, *the cocksucker.*"

As if I'm not confused enough. "Why would you say that about him?"

"You a reporter?" he snaps.

"No. Hardly."

"All the same, we're not supposed to talk about it. It was in all the papers at the time. Press has a ball with those kind of stories."

"I didn't live here then. What happened?"

"Let's just say the detective's not exactly missed around here."

"Why? I need to hear this. Please? This is very important to me."

"Because he almost single-handedly brought down this precinct, that's why."

I open my mouth to ask how, but he cuts me off. "Seriously, I can't talk about it. It's over with. And so is this conversation."

I begin walking away. Then something occurs to me, and I quickly turn back. "At least let me ask you this," I say. "Does it have anything to do with the murders at the Fálcon Hotel the other day?"

The officer looks at me with a completely blank stare. "What murders?"

And then—what can I say?—I faint.

Chapter 88

FIFTEEN OR TWENTY minutes later, still dazed and with another good-sized bump on my noggin, I walk a block before I even realize it's raining. I'm too busy replaying every single encounter with Detective Delmonico in my mind.

Is that where all of this has happened? In my mind?

It's impossible. Has to be.

I *talked* to him. He talked to me. He gave me his card. How does a dead man do that?

Wait a minute! Hold on!

I stop short in the middle of the sidewalk, the raindrops feeling icy cold against my face. Pulling Delmonico's card from my pocket, I rub it between my fingers just to prove to myself that it's real. It sure feels like it.

"Taxi!"

The first thing I do after rushing into my apartment is turn on my computer. I should be too freaked out, too bewildered to think straight. And yet the obsession to learn the truth about Delmonico—what happened and what *is* happening—has me focused like never before.

"It was in all the papers," said the cop at the precinct. Let's see about that.

I Google away, and the hits on Frank Delmonico's name number more than a thousand. Jeez, Louise! Some of the sites are the venomous rantings of bloggers, but most are indeed news stories—all archived—from the city's papers. The pages never turn yellow on the Internet.

I click on one site, then another and another. Not all of them include a picture, but when they do he's always wearing that same gray suit. His dark, intense eyes are unmistakable. It's him, all right. And each and every article confirms what I still can't bring myself to believe.

He's been dead for over three years.

The more I read, the more I realize why the police don't like talking about the guy. *Cocksucker,* indeed, and that's putting it mildly.

Delmonico was a highly decorated officer with over twenty years on the job. He was also on the take for at least ten of them.

And that's just for starters.

I keep clicking on sites until I find this one piece in the *New York Times* that lays the gory story out in grand detail. The article must be twenty-five hundred words.

Delmonico had gotten in bed with the Russian mob, protecting their interests in drugs and prostitution, as well as helping to launder money through the poker rooms of several Atlantic City casinos. The worst part was what happened when two young detectives from his precinct got close to linking one of his Russian comrades to a homicide in Queens. Delmonico whacked both detectives. Did the job himself.

What's more, he arranged it so he'd be the lead detective in the investigation. There was just one hitch. Delmonico thought they were alone in the alleyway when he pulled the trigger on the two detectives. He never saw an old Hasidic man who happened to be looking out a nearby tenement window. But the man in the window sure saw him.

Still, it seemed everyone thought Delmonico would get away with it—including most in the DA's office. It was the word of a veteran detective against that of an elderly man with admittedly bad eyesight. Speculation had it that the only reason the case went forward was that a nervous mayor didn't want to seem soft on police corruption, especially two cold-blooded murders.

But in the end, it was the Russians who proved even more nervous. A week before the start of the trial, Frank Delmonico was shot twice in the head at point-blank range. The gun used was a Makarov, a Russian-made 9 mm. Just in case that wasn't enough of a "message," there was something stuffed in Delmonico's mouth. *A big black rat.*

But that rat wasn't the real kicker.

At least from where I'm sitting.

Hoping to avoid the reporters and cameras camped outside his apartment in Queens, Delmonico had decided to check into a hotel. That's where they found his body.

At the Fálcon.

There was even a photo of his body being carried out in a long black bag.

Chapter 89

I STAND UP from my computer, having had more than enough of this. I'm woozy and in a daze. If Frank Delmonico's no longer alive, whom have I been talking to the past few days?

Impulsively, I reach into my pocket and pull out Delmonico's card. I think back to when he handed it to me outside the hotel. I can picture it clearly.

Wait.

That's it!

I rush to my darkroom and the pictures lining nearly every inch of wall space. I shot so many that morning outside the hotel. I covered every angle twice over. All the commotion. All the people. Police, paramedics—there's no way he could've escaped my lens.

Grabbing my loupe, I begin to search. It's my own desperate version of *Where's Waldo?* I move left to right across every photo, looking for that gray suit, those unmistakable eyes. *Where's Delmonico?*

I can't find him in any of the pictures.

So what do I do? I start over. I go slower, inch by inch,

top to bottom. The sweat from my face and arms is sticking to the photo paper. My head is throbbing; my eyes are killing me.

C'mon, where are you, Delmonico? I know you're here somewhere.

But he isn't.

Taking a giant step back, I breathe in deep and try to think. Dead or alive, real or imagined, what does Detective Frank Delmonico have to do with me? I'd never heard of him before, never seen him until that first time at the Fálcon. What does it mean that he wasn't there when the four bodies were carried out but afterward he was Frankie-on-the-spot, investigating me? That's something, but what does it mean?

Just then, I feel a pair of eyes on me and I nearly jump out of my skin.

Chapter 90

I TURN TO SEE my father staring down coldly from behind his thick glasses.

Next to the picture of him is the one of Dr. Magnumsen. They certainly have a connection with Delmonico. *They're dead.* At least they're supposed to be.

I study the image of my father on the streets of New York, his body such a startling contradiction: the square jaw versus the hunched shoulders; a strong man beaten down by an unfair world. My dad was a gifted carpenter, a volunteer fireman. Once, he rescued a little boy from a flooded ravine by tying a loop in his belt and hanging upside down from a bridge.

But being the town hero didn't pay well, and when his carpentry jobs started to dry up during the recession of the eighties, money in our house got tight. Ironic, really. He helped to build so many homes but ultimately couldn't afford to keep his own.

Maybe it wouldn't have been so bad had my mother been a little more understanding. She wasn't, though. I remember the night at the dinner table when she called him a failure in life, right to his face.

That's about when the drinking got out of control. But never in front of me. *Never.* I was his princess, his girl. No matter how bad things got, he always had a hug and a smile for me.

Right up until the end. Less than an hour before Dad shot himself in our dilapidated backyard shed, he held me in his arms and squeezed me tight. "It's going to be all right," he whispered in my ear.

I never forgave him for that lie. I know that I should've felt sorry for him, but I was too busy feeling sorry for myself.

Now, after all these years, he shows up somehow on a street corner in Manhattan. If only he hadn't run away that morning. I'd have given him the biggest hug and kiss, and whispered softly in his ear, "It's okay, Dad. I understand."

Chapter 91

I'M CRYING IN MY DARKROOM, the tears falling faster than I can wipe them away. I miss my dad. I miss a lot of things right now, but most of all my own sanity.

Could I be more of a mess?

It's late, and I've given up on trying to reach Michael tonight. I'm exhausted and should get some sleep.

But knowing that the dream—and God knows what else—awaits me in the morning, I instead reach for the shots I snapped of Penley and Stephen in front of the hotel.

Talk about a great Exhibit A.

In fact, it's enough to swing my mood. As I look at the first shot, I can't help relishing the thought of Michael going for the jugular in divorce court. I'm so giddy—or is it punchy?—I actually start singing, "Penley and Stephen in NYC, K-I-S-S-I-N-G!"

But the feeling is short-lived.

I stare at Stephen's transparent image—the exact same ghosting effect—and I surrender all faith in myself and in the real world as I experienced it before the last few days. I *know* I stood outside the Fálcon and watched those gurneys get wheeled to the curb, but I also know a pattern when I see one.

First *Penley*.

Then *Michael*.

Now *Stephen*.

One by one, the body bags are being accounted for, and I don't have to be Einstein to do the math.

There's one left.

Chapter 92

I COME OUT OF THE DARKROOM and notice there's a message on my answering machine—just one—and I'm afraid to listen to it. No, I'm *petrified* to press the button and hear what somebody has to tell me.

What now?

Who could this be? Another call from Kristin Burns?

I get a cold bottle of water in the kitchen and gulp it right down. *How did I get myself into this mess? How do I get out?*

There has to be a way, but I can't imagine what it might be. I'm supposed to be creative, aren't I? So why can't I begin to figure this puzzle out? Could anyone?

I can still see the red light flashing on my answering machine. It might be Michael, and maybe, *maybe* he's okay now, back to normal.

Of course, it could also be Delmonico, calling from *where,* exactly? Do they have phones there, wherever dead people hang out these days?

I approach the infernal message machine and I'm

starting to shake like a leaf. How insane is that? *Given what's happened to me?* Not so crazy.

I stab the button on the machine.

I get myself ready to listen to whomever, about whatever.

I hear a voice I don't know — a woman's voice. Who's this?

"Kristin . . . this is Leigh Abbott. I own the Abbott Show on Hudson Street, and I'm calling to tell you that we all love your stuff. Love it! Please give me a call at 212-555-6501. I would like to put your astounding work in the Abbott Show. Call me, Kristin: 212-555-6501. We are so impressed with your vision of New York."

I press the button on the machine again.

Listen to Leigh Abbott again.

It's the best news I've gotten since I moved to New York City. Absolutely the best by far. My dream has come true.

So — why am I crying uncontrollably?

Chapter 93

THE SOUND OF MY OWN SCREAM jolts my head off the pillow, piercing the still air of my bedroom like a jet engine on takeoff. I rip back the sheet in a panic, the sweat dripping from my hair.

I'm burning up—almost literally.

The dream's never been more real. It's getting worse.

I feel sick to my stomach and barely make it to the bathroom. I throw up so violently, my neck muscles convulse, cramping into knots. I begin to gag, then choke. Collapsing to the floor, I can't even call for help. *This is it, I'm going to die—on a cheapo bath mat from Bed Bath & Beyond!*

And the very last thing I'll hear is the music now starting to blare in my head.

Somehow, though, I keep breathing. What saves me is my lack of appetite last night. The stomach's barren; there's nothing left to get caught in my throat. I'm dry heaving and it hurts like crazy, but at least I'm alive.

Any other morning I'd be crawling back into bed, calling in sick. Instead, I take a shower and quickly get dressed. I don't have a choice. No free will at all. This is no time to be on the sidelines.

I try calling Michael at his office. The odds are he's arrived by now, but his line rings and rings and rings. It's too early for his secretary, Amanda. She doesn't normally get to her desk until around eight-thirty.

So I head off to Fifth Avenue, knowing no more about Michael's intentions than I did yesterday. Is he going to hurt somebody? Is he another Scott Peterson?

For the first time, I'm actually eager to see Penley. She needs to be okay. I certainly don't want her murdered. *My God, could it have happened already?* Is that why Michael isn't at work?

Chapter 94

"KRISTIN, IS THAT YOU?" I hear from down the hall as I step into the foyer of the Turnbulls' apartment.

"Yes, it's me."

And that's her. *Phew.* I instantly feel guilty about thinking the worst of Michael, putting him in the same company as a wife killer.

Penley turns the corner of the foyer and peers suspiciously at me. She's dressed in her "workout" clothes.

There's a moment as we eye each other, and it feels weird. So what else is new?

"Are you okay?" she asks. "You look a little pale, Kristin. You're not coming down with something, are you?"

"I'm fine. A little tired, I guess."

She gives me that "just us girls" smirk. "Late evening, huh?"

And a rough morning to boot. Of course, I'm not about to let on to anything, not with her. "No, it was pretty quiet," I say.

"That reminds me. Maria said you called last night. Did you need to talk to me about something?"

Thanks, Maria!

I hesitate, thinking fast.

"Oh, that," I say. "It was a false alarm. I thought I'd left my cell phone here."

She seems to buy it, nodding anyway. This is some game we're playing here, the Pencil and I.

"By the way, how was your dinner?" I ask.

"Pardon?" *Point, Kristin.*

"You and Mr. Turnbull. Maria told me you went out to dinner. Just the two of you?"

"Yes. It was very nice, thank you," she says. "We don't do it enough. The two of us, no kids." *Point, Pencil.*

"Is he at his office now?"

As soon as the question leaves my lips, I regret it. I've never asked her where Michael is; why would I now? *Dumb, dumb, dumb.*

Sure enough, Penley gives me a quizzical look. "Where else would he be?"

Chapter 95

IT'S A VERY GOOD, very logical question and just about the only thing I'm thinking about as I walk Dakota and Sean to school.

That is, until Sean interrupts me with one of his own questions. A real doozy too.

"Miss Kristin, am I going to die?"

I'm stunned. By the question and its timing. *Why ask that now, Sean?*

The sweetness in his voice brings a lump to my throat. For the second time this morning, I can barely breathe.

I try to fake a reassuring smile for him. "Sean, honey, why would you ask that?"

"Because Timmy Rockwell at school said I was going to die. Dakota too. Is he right?"

I need to be careful how I answer. Five-year-olds can be so impressionable. I don't want to scare him, but I also don't want to lie.

In the meantime, Dakota couldn't care less either way. Seven-year-olds have no need for tact. "Everybody dies, stupid!" she says.

Sean squeezes my hand hard. I can feel how frightened he is about this.

"Is that true, Miss Kristin? Does everybody die?"

I stop walking and kneel down, pulling the two of them close to me. "No one gets to live forever, Sean. But you don't have to be scared, because you're going to be alive for a very, very long and wonderful time."

He blinks slowly. "Really? I am? And Mommy and Daddy? And you, Miss Kristin?"

"Yes, of course. And that goes for you too, princess," I say, giving Dakota a poke in the belly.

"What about Timmy Rockwell?" asks Sean. "He's mean, so will he die sooner?"

I smile. "It doesn't quite work like that. Mean has nothing to do with it."

"It should," he says.

I throw my arms around them both again, and for a moment the island of Manhattan is just the three of us. *Three*. A much better number than four.

"Okay, c'mon," I say, standing up. "We're going to be late for school, and *that* is *unacceptable*."

I grab their hands—but I don't walk a step.

"What's wrong, Miss Kristin?" asks Sean.

"Yeah," says Dakota. "Why aren't we moving?"

The answer is staring at us from across the street. We're no longer alone.

The Ponytail is back.

"Hey!" I yell. "Hey! You! Hey, I'm talking to you."

Where I get the courage—or is it stupidity?—to bark at a guy who's been scaring the bejesus out of me, I don't know. That is him, though, isn't it?

He ducks around the corner, but yes, I'm almost sure

that's who it was. I'd be even surer if there hadn't been something blocking his face.

Of all things . . . *a camera.*

"Are you okay, Miss Kristin?" asks Dakota, showing real concern. "Who was that? He looked scary."

"Nobody, nothing . . . Yeah, I'm fine, honey," I say. "Let's get going."

I want to run but I know I can't. Not with the kids in tow. So we walk. Nice and easy, as we always do.

The only difference is that I'm looking back over my shoulder every ten seconds or so, a nervous wreck again.

Where are you, Ponytail?

What do you want?

With me?

With these kids?

What's with the camera?

Chapter 96

THERE'S NO SIGN of the Ponytail and his camera now. Not on crowded Fifth Avenue. Not along Madison, not in front of the gates of the Preston Academy. I've got one sore and twisted neck to prove it.

I hug Sean and Dakota again, extra hard. I don't want to let go. "I'll see you right here this afternoon. Like always, okay?"

"Are you sure everything's all right?" asks Dakota. "Are you sure, Miss Kristin?" She looks worried. About *me*. It's sweet.

"Sure, I'm sure! Never been better," I boast, forcing a bright smile. "Now, go have a great day!"

I don't bother with a wink and neither do the kids. I just don't have any cuteness in me today.

They both nod their little heads and scamper off across the tree-lined courtyard, bounding up the stone front steps to the school. So many mornings I've stood watching Dakota and Sean from this exact spot.

I'm about to turn away when I see them stop on the

top step and look back. In unison, they wave to me, their smiles curled wide.

I want to cry, and I almost do. But I just wave in return, fighting back the tears.

With them safely inside, the tears come. Then I do one more three sixty, searching for the Ponytail.

Still don't see him. The bastard. The creep. Is he dead too—like Delmonico?

Out of nowhere, the song is back in my head. I even catch a word, or I think I do—*game?* "What is that goddamn song?" I mutter as a couple of passersby stare at me.

I wipe my eyes dry, then check my watch while reaching for my cell phone. *It's high time I track down that other disappearing man in my life.*

At the very least, Michael's secretary will be there now to answer my call. And after three rings, she picks up.

"Michael Turnbull's office."

"Hi, is he there, please?"

"May I ask who's calling?"

"This is Kristin Burns. The Turnbulls' nanny? Is this Amanda?"

"Yes, hi, Kristin," she says. "I take it you're not at their home, are you?"

"No, why do you ask?"

"Mr. Turnbull said he tried calling to see if anyone was there. It turns out he left some important papers in his library. I guess he was hoping you or his wife could bring them to him."

"I could do that. I'm heading back there now. I just dropped off Dakota and Sean at school."

"I'm afraid he already left to get the papers himself.

He needs them for a meeting later this morning. If you're on your way there, I suppose you might see him."

Yes! At last, the possibility of a good break. Before Amanda even finishes the sentence, I've got my arm raised for a taxi that's just dropped off some older kids at the school.

Less than ten minutes later, I'm on the elevator heading up to the penthouse. I'm so relieved I might be seeing Michael that I forget how mad he's made me these past twenty-four hours. All is forgiven, but now we need to talk, seriously talk.

I step into the foyer and right away I hear his voice. A little muffled. I think it's coming from the kitchen. *Who's Michael talking to?*

Chapter 97

I CAN'T EXACTLY MAKE OUT his words as I tiptoe back through the dining room. It's definitely Michael, though.

I press my ear against the swinging door to the kitchen. There's something different about his voice, a slight echo. And then I realize who he's talking to.

The answering machine.

I push through the door into the empty kitchen and spy the blinking red light. Michael is midsentence in the message he's leaving, and I listen for a moment to what he's saying. It's *good-bye,* that's what. He's about to hang up.

"I'll see you later, then, okay, honey? I love you," he says. "Love you."

I dash to the phone, but it's too late.

Click.

He had to be calling from his cell. Is he still on his way here? I immediately start dialing it when my finger stops. Something doesn't make sense.

What did he say?

I love you? . . . Love you?

He couldn't have left the message for me, of course. It had to be for Penley. Is he trying to keep up appearances with her? As cool and clever as Michael can be, I find that hard to believe. He hates her too much right now.

The answering machine continues to blink, practically begging me to play back the entire message. *Go ahead, Kris. Satisfy your curiosity.*

I hesitate only because I'm not supposed to—listen to messages, that is. One of the first things Penley told me when I started the job was that I "needn't concern myself with the machine." Translation: *keep your nose out of my business!*

So for the past two years, I've not once hit the playback button.

Until now.

Screw it, what have I got to lose? My job? One way or the other, I don't think I'll be the nanny here for much longer. All the more reason to listen to the message. I don't like how it ended.

Besides, didn't Amanda say that Michael had already called earlier? The timing seems strange.

So I hit the button. "You have one new message," says the automated voice.

"Hi, honey, it's me," Michael begins. He sounds somber, almost crestfallen.

Then he absolutely blows my mind.

Chapter 98

I CAN'T BREATHE as I listen to Michael's words. It's almost as if I'm hearing them one at a time.

"I've obviously been doing a lot of thinking since last night. That was pretty clever, by the way, your bringing me to our favorite restaurant to break the news. God knows how I would've reacted if we weren't in public.

"Maybe that's the problem; you know me too well. Because right now, I feel as if I have no idea who you are. Oh, Christ, that sounds like some cheesy movie line, doesn't it?

"I know I'm not the easiest guy to be married to, and I know what you told me took guts—and you probably wouldn't have said anything unless you really do want us to work things out. But the whole thing, I mean, it just came as such a shock.

"Shit. I don't want to say something here I'm going to regret, but you've got to understand how upset I am. You keep saying that you love me and, yes, I love you, but I don't know if that's going to be enough. I guess we'll have to see.

"One other thing, though—I'm a little worried about your wanting to end things with this guy in person. What if he doesn't take the news well? I want to make sure you know what you're doing. Think about it, Penley. Okay?

"I don't know; maybe I'm just being paranoid. Hopefully, you'll do the same thing you did with me and take him to a restaurant. Jeez, this is too weird. I'm actually giving advice to my wife on how to end her affair.

"You know what? I'm going to leave the office and head home. It's not like I'm getting any work done here. In fact, I think I'm going to pick up some ice cream along the way. Chunky Monkey, of course. To hell with the diets, right?

"So if you hear this message before I get there, hang around, okay? We'll pig out and do some more talking.

"I'll see you later, then, okay, honey? I love you. . . . Love you."

I stand there motionless in the kitchen while my brain goes absolutely haywire.

I can't believe Penley would confess to her affair.

And I also can't believe Michael would ever consider forgiving her, let alone discuss staying together. Has he been stringing me along this entire time? Is there a whole plotline going on that I'm not aware of?

I'm so confused, I don't know which end is up. It's all one big hazy cloud. Plus, I think I'm going to be sick. Reaching a hand out to the counter, I try to steady myself. I need to figure this out. *Think, Kristin, think!*

It just doesn't feel right. Michael sounded too meek on the phone.

Unassuming.

Docile.

Harmless.

Innocent.

And then it all becomes clear to me.

Everything does.

From the beginning right up until Michael's message.

Or, should I say, his alibi.

I turn and rush to the fridge, pulling open the freezer door.

There, staring back at me, is a brand-new pint of Ben & Jerry's ice cream. Chunky Monkey, of course.

God is in the details.

Chapter 99

"CAN'T YOU GO any faster?"

The cabbie glares back at me, pissed. "Hey, I'm going as fast as I can, lady!"

"No, you're not! And this is a matter of life and death."

"What? You're late for your *Pilates* class?"

He's speeding down Fifth Avenue, probably looking to cut over to Madison. We're still blocks away from the Fálcon.

It's come down to this. I don't understand anything completely, and yet it all makes sense. Finally. I've never been surer of anything in my life. It's up to me. It's *always* been up to me. If I don't get to the hotel in time, something horrible is going to happen.

I've seen it happen.

And at this very moment, all I can do is wonder. Will I be too late?

The cab careens around a corner. *Now we're cooking! Fuck.*

Traffic! A parking-lot situation.

The driver skids to a halt behind another cab, a Checker, sandwiched in by a city bus that's blowing hot smoke.

"Here!" I say, pushing money through the divider. "Take it. Keep the change!"

"Hope you make your class, sweetheart."

I bolt from the backseat and start running, my heart pounding as fast as my feet are moving. And I'm so scared.

Why, Michael, why? Don't throw everything away. Don't throw us away. Or the kids.

All I can see in my head are the images from the hotel, what was in my dream and what I captured on film. The procession of gurneys being wheeled out. And then—I think of my other time at the Fálcon. Three years ago with Boston Matthew. Coincidence? I doubt it. But I don't want to think about it now. I couldn't if I wanted to.

Hurry! Just hurry.

Stay in the moment.

I hear a siren warbling up ahead, and my heart sinks, my legs actually buckle, and I nearly fall.

I'm too late. I blew it.

No—it's a fire engine heading downtown, a blur of red shooting by a block away on Madison. The blare of the siren trails off, restoring hope. What is with the Fálcon Hotel, anyway?

I'm almost there. The burn from my legs is moving up to my lungs. It feels like a load of bricks has been dumped on my chest. But I don't dare stop running. Nothing can make me stop.

Then, something does.

Chapter 100

MY CELL PHONE RINGS.

Michael! This has to be him!

I cut sharply to my right on the sidewalk, pulling up alongside a building. Barely able to catch my breath, I answer the phone.

"Hello?"

It's not him.

"Is this Kristin Burns?" I hear. It's a woman. I don't recognize the voice, but she sounds upset. *Oh man, this is no time for more pranks from the dark side.*

"Yes."

"This is Madeline Sturges from Preston Academy. I've tried to reach *both* Mr. and Mrs. Turnbull. To no avail. And you're listed here as another contact —"

"What's wrong?" I interrupt.

There's a silence, and I can practically feel the woman's anxiety through the phone. "It's Dakota," she says. "She told a classmate that she needed to go find someone."

"What? I don't understand."

"She's missing from school. We've looked everywhere. Dakota's gone."

The phone drops from my hand. Before it hits the sidewalk, I'm sprinting again. Faster than ever.

Four gurneys.

Please, God. Don't let this happen. Not to Dakota. She's only seven years old.

How could she know about the Fálcon or that her mother might be there? It doesn't seem possible.

Yeah, just like everything else that's happened so far.

The pathetic truth is—anything is possible right now.

Chapter 101

I'M CLOSE. The corner of the Fálcon is twenty . . . ten . . . five feet away. I squeeze my eyes shut, running blind. I can't bear to look at this.

But I have to look, don't I? I feel like I have no free will in this matter.

Racing around the corner, I brace for the worst shock of my life. *The four body bags.*

They aren't there, thank God. Not yet, at least.

There's no crime scene, no throng of onlookers. No Dakota either. Just the bright red awning of the Fálcon, pulling me in with its powerful undertow.

Seconds later, I burst through the front doors. *Don't let them be in the same room as before!* It's where Michael would surely look first. He knows the number. I told him.

Dashing through the lobby, I head straight for the elevators, only to see half a dozen people waiting there. Without breaking stride, I turn for the stairs, taking two at a time. I'm leaking buckets of sweat as I climb past the second and third floors.

Spilling out onto the fourth, I practically hurl myself down the long hallway.

It's quiet.

Too quiet.

Never has a silence sounded so deadly, so haunting and eerie.

I pass one door after another until I reach the room Penley and Stephen were in. *Their room.* I come to a fast stop, and it's as if I've given the pain of running here a chance to catch up. My legs and lungs feel like an inferno.

I see a "Do Not Disturb" sign that wasn't there yesterday. Staring at it, I almost don't notice the other thing that's different.

The door's open.

Just an inch, not even that. A small sliver of space between the door and the jamb. Slowly, I push my way in.

It's no Motel 6. The room is more of a chic apartment. I step into a foyer with black-and-white tile like a chessboard. *More games to play?* For the first time, I hear something—a voice from around the corner.

It's Stephen.

Is he laughing? Why would he be laughing?

I take a few more steps forward and realize he isn't laughing. No, he's crying. Sobbing is more like it.

Peeking my head out, I glimpse down the short hallway and I see why.

Michael has a gun pressed to his forehead.

Chapter 102

"PLEASE, DON'T DO THIS," begs Stephen in a high-pitched whine. "Please, no! Please!" He's naked, quivering and cowering by the foot of the bed. It's all I can see in the dim room.

"Shut up!" barks Michael. "Shut the hell up!"

It's happening so fast, and I'm frozen, almost as if I'm stuck in time or I'm watching a dream. That hideous burning smell is back too.

Michael cocks the gun, his voice seared with rage. "You fucked the wrong woman, and you *definitely* fucked with the wrong guy," he says to Stephen. Then —

PFFTT!

I see the spurt of blood even before I hear the strange muffled blast.

The back of Stephen's head blows out, and the wall behind him is splattered with dark red brain matter. For a second, he remains standing, his eyes open and brimming with terror. A flap of scalp juts out behind his ear like an open gate. *This isn't a dream, Kris.*

Then Stephen's body goes limp, as if a puppeteer suddenly released the strings. His arms and legs fold as he melts to the floor, a pool of blood around his head creeping wider and wider. The blood on the floor looks almost black.

God is in the details, right?

I begin to scream, just like in my dream.

Michael whirls around, his arm outstretched, the gun aimed right at me. Watching his gloved trigger finger twitch, I throw out my hands. "NO! MICHAEL! IT'S ME!"

He squints, seeing that it's true. It is me.

"What are you doing here?" he says, lowering the gun.

I struggle for words, but there aren't any up to the task. All I can do is slowly walk toward him. I'm not sure if I want to hold him or hit him.

"Don't touch anything!" he says. It's an order.

Huh?

"Fingerprints," he explains. "Ours can't be here. Don't touch a thing."

He begins twisting a small tube off the gun's barrel—a silencer, I assume. That's why the blast wasn't really much of a blast.

Then he stops, thinks for a split second, changes his mind. Twist, twist, twist. The silencer stays on.

That's the word for this, isn't it? *Twisted.*

I keep moving toward him, my body feeling as if it's crumbling with each step. Words finally come. "What have you done, Michael?"

That's when I look farther into the bedroom and realize—*I only knew half of it.*

Michael slaps his hand over my mouth before I can

scream again. Keeled over on a desk by the bed is a very naked, very dead Penley, blood still dripping down her chest and leg. An awful lot of blood is pooled on the floor.

Michael removes the hand from my mouth, raising a finger to his. "*Shhh,* we don't have a lot of time," he says. "We have to leave now. Kristin, we'll be fine."

He's so cool as he pulls a silk kerchief from his suit pocket and wipes the gun clean. Kneeling down, he places the gun in Stephen's hand. Then he does something I don't understand at all. Michael wipes the back of his own hand on Stephen's fingers, wrist, and forearm.

I watch it all in total shock.

Michael seems so eerily calm, almost robotic as he works. He could just as easily be making a ham sandwich as *framing* another man for a murder-suicide.

What did he say about Stephen on the answering machine? *"What if he doesn't take the news well?"*

Michael stands up, scowling at me, and it's as if I've never seen him before in my life.

"You weren't supposed to be here," he says.

Were that only true. But I know otherwise. I was definitely meant to see this; I just don't understand *why* yet.

"Where did you get the gun?" I ask.

"It doesn't matter."

I think I know. "Vincent gave it to you?"

Michael nods. "He's parked downstairs. Around the corner. He'll take us home, and we'll wait for the police to contact me. You and I have a lot of acting to do, Kristin."

Chapter 103

I BARELY HEAR MICHAEL as my legs turn to rubber. I'm feeling dizzy and faint. I'm his accomplice now, aren't I? An accomplice to a double murder. But I didn't do anything. I came here to stop Michael, not to help him.

He grabs my shoulders, giving me a hard shake. "Stay with me now, okay? *You've got to stay with me, Kristin.* We're going to be okay."

This doesn't seem like the time or place for a heartfelt confession, and yet it's perfect, somehow.

"I have something I need to tell you," I say.

"Not right now. *Not* now!"

"Yes. Right now, right here. Three years ago —"

"Kris, shut up! Just *shut up!*"

"Three years ago, I was pregnant and about to have a baby, Michael. I came to New York with my boyfriend, who was the baby's father.

"I had the baby *right here in this hotel,* Michael. Don't you see? Don't you get it? It all revolves around this place, whatever *it* is. My boyfriend, Matthew, was pre-med at

Tufts. He delivered the baby, a little boy like Sean, right here. We had agreed to leave the baby at a hospital after it was born. But the baby, the little boy died. Right here at the Fálcon. Can you imagine what that was like? I let my baby die, Michael! I saw my baby die, my little boy."

Now it's Michael's turn to look and wonder if he knows who I am. It's a dilemma I've been facing myself, for three years.

"We have to go," he says.

I stare back into his eyes, if only because I can't bear to look anywhere else in the room. Not at blown-away Stephen, not at Penley—*definitely* not at Penley.

He really did it. *He killed her.*

"Everything's going to be okay," he says as we head for the door. "We're done here."

But not by my count. Not even close.

All along I've been seeing four gurneys. Stephen and Penley only make two. Two dead. *So we're not quite done here, are we?*

"Wait," I say, stopping. "What was that noise?"

Make that *one* dead.

Chapter 104

"SURPRISE, YOU BASTARD!"

I spin around to see a knife plunging into Michael's neck. Once, twice, Penley stabs him before he even knows what's happened.

Payback, that's what.

Michael grabs for his throat with both hands as a red river gushes down past his collar, soaking his shirt in an instant. His mouth opens, but the only sound I hear is the gurgling of his blood.

She keeps stabbing him. Three, four times. *This isn't Penley; it's a killer possessed.* Again and again, the silver of the blade disappears into Michael's flesh — the neck, the chest, the shoulders — he can barely lift a hand to try and stop her.

And she's not about to stop on her own.

I lunge at Penley, desperately reaching for her pumping arm. She's so much smaller than me — *she's been shot, for Christ's sake!* — and still she pushes me away as if I'm nothing. Of course, that's what I've always been to her.

Am I next? I wonder.

I turn and see Stephen's bloody and bare-assed body sprawled on the carpet. My eyes move from his shattered head down to his arm, until I arrive at his outstretched hand.

The gun!

I'm scrambling now, making this up as I go along. Just trying to survive is all it is. I'm half running, half crawling, anything to get me to that gun.

Behind me, Michael's body crashes to the floor with a resounding *thud!* He's wheezing and gasping for air, and I realize that I still love him, and that he's dying.

As my fingers stretch for the gun, I hear Penley's voice over my shoulder.

"Oh, no, you don't!"

I yank the gun out of Stephen's cold grip and whip around, fumbling for the trigger. Penley is charging right at me.

"YOU PIECE OF SHIT!" she yells, and she doesn't sound anything like her old self. Strange, but in a way, I like the *new* Penley a little better.

She raises her arm high, her elbow cocked and ready to pounce, that is, *stab*. The blade is covered with Michael's blood, and now she wants mine on it too.

I close my eyes.

Then immediately open them again.

Don't think, just shoot.

Chapter 105

PFFTT.

Pfftt.

Those sounds may be strange, but they're deadly.

Penley folds in two and collapses right in front of me. The knife in her hand slices down inches from my face. The first bullet struck her in the chest; the second, the right side of her forehead.

I look at the knife, wondering how she would have one in her possession.

She didn't.

It's a letter opener. Suffice to say, the kind they would never let you bring on an airplane. Long and sharp. On the sleek silver handle I can see engraved lettering: "The Fálcon Hotel."

Nice touch.

I struggle fiercely to rise to my feet, emptying my lungs with just about the deepest exhale of my life. But the relief is short. I look at Michael, then hurry over to him. He's facedown. His breath is coming in short gasps that seem very painful.

"Michael, can you hear me?"

He blinks slowly, his eyes searching. "Kris?"

His voice is so weak, and he's coughing blood onto the rug.

"I'm right here," I say. "I'm going to get help for you."

But I think we both know he's beyond that. Michael's neck and chest are shredded, a gory multitude of stab wounds. He's lost so much blood already, it's a wonder he can speak.

"You have to get out of here," he says. "The police . . ."

"It's okay. It's okay."

He's fading on me, struggling to talk. "No, you need to hurry. Run. Get away from here."

Where? Where do I go?

Michael spells it out with his last breath, his final words to me.

"The kids," he whispers.

His eyes go wide.

"Michael!" I yell. "Michael!"

But he's gone.

Michael's dead.

And instantly I realize—that makes three bodies.

Chapter 106

I STAND UP SLOWLY, taking one last look at Michael, and it hits me — *what I'm seeing right now.*

It's the picture of Michael from my camera. The shot of him sprawled dead on a floor somewhere.

The one I never took.

Yet here it is. Here I am. How could this happen?

It feels as if I've been hit with a stun gun. Time has stopped completely. The world has stopped. All that continues is the deadly — really, truly deadly — silence.

Then it's broken.

The phone by the bed rings, then rings a second time, snapping me out of it. *I need to get out of here. To get away!*

I bolt from the room and head toward the back stairs. I know the way out of here. I'm halfway to the stairwell when I hear footsteps pounding behind me.

The kids!

Could it be? *Dakota?* If not — then who? I'm almost afraid to find out.

But I stop and spin around to look. And it's not her.

It's *him*.

The Ponytail.

How could *he* be here? How does he fit into this? I want to ask him. But not now!

Oh, dear God! Oh, no!

As in — *that's no camera he's wielding.*

"Freeze!" he yells, taking aim at me.

I thrust out my hands in a panic — *Don't shoot!* — only to realize immediately I've made a mistake. There's one thing I forgot to do back in the hotel room, before I charged out of there on my getaway run.

Let go of the gun.

Chapter 107

THIS IS WHAT HAPPENS in the next instant—*I die.*

I don't feel the bullet as it rips through my body. I'm not even sure I'm shot until I look down and see the bloodstain.

Slowly, I rub the palm of my hand across my shirt. It feels warm, sticky, unreal.

He thought I was going to shoot him. Ridiculous! Except I just shot Penley, didn't I?

I stumble back a step before my legs give out. Now I'm spinning—at least that's the feeling I have. I fall hard to the floor, but I don't feel the impact.

I don't feel anything, really, and in some ways that's an improvement.

I'm lying faceup, gazing at the hallway ceiling. A shiny "Exit" sign points to the stairs I never reached. Other than that, it's a blank picture.

Then a face appears.

The Ponytail hovers over me. He looks at the gun clenched in my hand and ruefully shakes his head. Bending down, he presses two fingers against the side of my neck. What's he doing? Oh, I see, he's feeling for a pulse.

"I'm still alive," I say.

He doesn't respond in any way. Nothing.

"Hey, did you hear me? Who are you, anyway?" I ask.

He stands there and takes out a cell phone, dialing 911. I get my answer.

"I'm a private investigator," he tells the operator after reporting there's been a shooting. "*Multiple* shootings," he corrects himself.

The police arrive, followed by EMS. Lots of hustle and bustle all around me. A paramedic checks my pulse again.

I fade in and out for a while, then I hear the Ponytail explain to a cop that he was hired by "one of the deceased." Mrs. Penley Turnbull was his client.

"She suspected her husband was having an affair," he says. "Apparently the husband suspected the same thing about her."

"Hope you got paid up-front," jokes the cop.

"You think this is funny?" I say.

He doesn't hear me. No one does.

"So, who's the girl?"

The cop is pointing at me. When is this strangeness going to stop? Actually, when I think about it, I don't want it to stop, do I?

"The nanny," answers the Ponytail. "That's who I discovered the husband was involved with."

"So you were following her? If I'm following *you* so far?"

"Yeah, you got it right. Mrs. Turnbull wanted to see if

I could dig up any dirt on her, I guess for the divorce. I kind of felt sorry for her, though. Kristin's her name. She was young, in way over her head. I even tried scaring the shit out of her, hoping she'd back off the relationship with the husband, who's a real scumbag."

"Instead, here she is with a gun," says the cop. "She had to be in on it with the husband, right?"

"I'm not so sure," says the Ponytail. "I lost her at first when she entered the hotel, but the way she ran here, I think maybe she was trying to stop this from happening."

The cop sighs. "Damn shame either way. There's two little kids now with no mommy and daddy."

"Or even a nanny. I could tell the kids liked her a lot."

"That would explain it," the cop says with a nod and a shrug.

"What's that?"

"We sent a patrol car over to their school to get them, and the daughter was missing. Seven years old. I got word a minute ago, though, that they found her."

"Alive?"

"Oh, yeah. She's fine. In a manner of speaking."

"Where was she?"

"Home. The little girl said she ditched school because she was worried about the nanny. She wanted to be with her."

"Her name's Dakota. Did she know something?"

"She claims she didn't. Just had a bad feeling. Of course, when she arrived home, no one was there. They were all *here*."

As the two of them walk away, all I can think about is Dakota and Sean. I need to be with them. Someone does. Little Sean's going to have so many questions.

I scream out again to no avail. Why can't anyone hear me? I continue to scream, just like in the dream.

Am I already dead? I wonder.

But I can see. I can hear.

What the hell's going on?

"Exactly," comes a voice that I recognize.

Chapter 108

I SEE HIS WARPED reflection in the exit sign, and it makes me shudder. He's standing in the doorway right next to me. Looking like the creep of all creeps.

Frank Delmonico.

He steps into the hallway. Behind him, in the room he came out of, is nothing but darkness.

And the music from my dream.

It's the same room! The one I was banging on the door of yesterday.

But nobody answered.

The music engulfs me now, it's so intense. And for the first time since the song took root in my head like a horrible weed, there's something more.

Words.

And the seasons they go round and round,
And the painted ponies go up and down.
We're captive on the carousel of time.

Delmonico stands directly over me, wearing the same gray suit. Cops walk by, but they don't seem to notice him.

"Hello, Kristin," he says. "I know, I know, you're innocent. You didn't do anything to deserve this."

"This is impossible," I blurt out. "You're dead."

"So they say. I've been sent to look after you anyway. To talk to you. Kind of an interview. What do they call them in the business world—exit interviews?" He reaches into his jacket and pulls out a pack of cigarettes.

And go round and round and round, I hear the
    music continue.
In the circle game.

Delmonico lights up. He winks at me before blowing out the match. Except there is no match, just the flame. How did he do that?

I squeeze my eyes shut. *It's all a dream,* I tell myself. *It has to be.*

"No," says Delmonico. "It was never a dream, Kristin."

"Then there's been a mistake. I'm not like you. You killed people."

"You killed too. Don't you remember?"

"That was different."

"You're right. That's the thing about life; it's not always so black and white." He takes a long drag off his cigarette.

I feel something on my leg. It's moving up my thigh, across my stomach.

"Get it off of me!"

Whatever it is, it climbs up my neck, onto my face. It crawls right past my mouth, over my eyes. Now I can see it! I'm screaming, terrified. It's the biggest cockroach ever.

Delmonico raises his foot high. The heel of his shoe comes crashing down next to my head.

Crunch!

"As I said, Kristin, this is an interview."

"An interview for what?" I ask.

"Well, to see where you fit in. You say you're innocent, and yet you had that terrible affair with a married man. You've been self-centered for most of your life. And then there's your poor little baby boy. Dead. Your fault. Yours and Matthew's. Right here at the Fálcon. How could you?"

I stare at him, horrified that he knows everything. "What is this place, anyway?"

He sighs. "It's where *I* died, for one thing, so that gets me a little sentimental, y'know. It's a portal, Kristin, a gateway. To you-know-where. There are several of them in this big, bad city of New York. But listen to me rattle on. I'm doing all the talking here—and this is *your* day, Kristin."

Chapter 109

I'M STARTING TO FEEL very afraid now, and I'm nauseated as well. I smell something burning again. Hives all over my body? Who knows? I have so many questions, I don't know where to start.

I hear this *slap, slap, slap* — and I see that Delmonico is tapping his foot beside my head.

"I don't have all day for this, missy. I should say, *you* don't have a lot of time left."

"For my interview?"

"Exactly. So talk to me. It's almost time to go. We have to leave these hallowed halls."

"*Go where?* Where am I going?"

"Oh, you know as well as I do. What is this you're trying — *the stupidity defense?* 'I'm not accountable because I'm dense?' You're not so dumb, Kristin. Boston College. Prelaw. Well, that wasn't such a great choice, was it?"

"So the Fálcon Hotel is the portal, one of the gates — to my destination?"

Delmonico isn't pleased. "I believe we've covered that ground already. But *yes.*"

I can barely speak. "Because? . . . I've made some terrible mistakes?"

"To put it mildly, yes. You've been a bad, bad girl. Like so many of your kind."

My throat feels as if it's closing up on me, but I still manage the next few words.

"Am I . . . a devil?"

At this, Delmonico has a hearty laugh. "Oh, you wish," he says.

He sighs out loud, then starts to talk again.

"Here's a way that might help you understand what's going to happen to you. Growing up, in Brooklyn this was—near where you met up with the guy with the ponytail, actually—I went to Catholic grade school. I'll never forget this one. Parish priest gives an inspirational talk to our class. Sixth grade, I think it was. The talk is all about eternity, eternal damnation, and how to comprehend it, as if that's possible. The priest says, 'Imagine there's this tiny little blackbird, lives on a huge mountain in upstate New York or some other godforsaken place. And every thousand years, that little bird fills its beak with whatever it can carry and flies down to Brooklyn and deposits its mouthful in our school parking lot. Now, imagine that the blackbird does this until the entire mountain has been transported there. And *that,* ladies and gentlemen, would be just the *beginning* of eternity.'

"Here's another thought for you. This whole nightmare, all of it, it's been going on for about thirteen seconds. *Start to finish,* thirteen seconds. Count 'em—thirteen. So do you see how horrible an eternity of this would be?"

All of what has happened so far . . . it's taken thirteen seconds? My God!

Delmonico flicks the ash of his cigarette, and some of it drifts down onto me.

"But what's going to happen to me for eternity?" I ask.

"The dumb defense again. I love it," Delmonico says and laughs. "Oh, you'll see. You'll find out soon enough. That's a good one, missy. *What happens next.* How's this for a sneak preview?"

Delmonico opens his mouth wider than I've ever seen a human mouth open. And then a rat sticks its furry head out the opening. The vermin looks at me, then it disappears back inside Delmonico. "Yum," he says.

He laughs and laughs, and a smoke ring he blows floats over my head as he turns and walks back into the room, and the darkness.

"Is that the portal to hell in there?" I call to him. "Is it? Delmonico?"

Just then, though, a policewoman leans in very close to me, and I wonder if she's going to move me somewhere.

But then—*don't think, just shoot*—she takes my picture.

Chapter 110

TWO PARAMEDICS ROLL OUT a long plastic bag next to my body, zipper side up.

"Stop!" I plead. "*I'm not dead!* Please, please, won't you stop?"

They raise my arms to tuck them in close to my sides, and I glimpse the blood dripping from my right hand.

"One, two, three," they count. Then they lift me and deposit me into a body bag.

My God, my God, please, no. Don't do this!

They close the zipper even as I continue to beg them not to do it, to give me a second chance for some reason that isn't even clear to me.

I've never felt more helpless, more frightened or *alone*.

As they wheel me down the hall, into the elevator, and across the lobby, I stare out in horror and dread. Through the dark, dingy plastic, everything looks gray.

Even the red awning as I'm taken out of the hotel.

They push me toward the curb, the wheels of the gurney squeaking like sick birds as they spin against the pavement.

I listen to the murmuring of the crowd that's gathered outside on the street. They're wondering what happened.

Who died in there?

I keep screaming, "There's been a horrible mistake. I'm not dead!"

But no one hears me.

Not the businessman in his pinstripe suit, the bike messenger, or the mother with her stroller, the same ones I saw in my dream. The strangers . . . who are now attending my funeral, so to speak.

I'm so scared now.

Please, God, make it stop! Please, God, please, God!

But he can't hear me either.

Or worse, maybe he can and just doesn't care about Kristin Burns.

Overhead, all I see are the police and EMS lights spinning against the buildings.

"Somebody do something! Get me out of here! Please! Somebody!"

The zipper to the body bag is inches from my eyes. It's so close, but it might as well be miles away. I can't reach it.

I can't move.

But then the zipper starts to open — jarred, perhaps, by a crack in the sidewalk.

And that's when I hear it — out on the street, pushing through the crowd — someone desperately screaming as loud as I am. The voice is thick with panic.

"HELP! THAT PERSON IS ALIVE!"

Closer and closer comes the voice, until the moment arrives when I see the face behind it, and all hope dies.

The horror comes full circle. The woman screaming outside the hotel?

She's me!

And I understand everything.

In a few minutes, very soon, the dream will start again. I'll wake up in my bed, screaming. I'll hear the song. I'll hear the knocking at my door. Mrs. Rosencrantz will be there.

And I will keep reliving these horrifying last days, over and over, until the tiny blackbird has transported that mountain, a beakful at a time, one trip every thousand years.

Only that will just be the beginning of eternity.

In you-know-where.

And I'm screaming, screaming, screaming, screaming . . .

Chapter 111

SO HERE I AM on my way to hell. As I understand it from Delmonico, I'll keep reliving some version of the nightmare I've just experienced for eternity, for life everlasting. Definitely something to look forward to.

I can see around me clearly now, since nobody has bothered to rezip my body bag.

Actually, I'm glad of that. I get one last look around, and everything seems kind of strangely beautiful about the world, actually. The light is gauzy, with streaks of burnt orange and yellow laced through it. The faces of the people watching are actually sad, almost as if they care, and that touches me.

I want to cry, but I can't really control my body anymore, can I? I wonder how much longer I have—until everything goes black or white or until this horrifying nightmare starts all over again.

And again.

And again.

How much time, Kris?

And how much time did I waste in my life? How many things did I do all wrong? Would I do them differently now?

I think I would. Honestly, and this isn't a cop-out, I know I would live a different life. I feel so guilty . . . about my baby . . . about the affair with Michael . . . about hurting Dakota and Sean . . . even about hurting Penley, who was a twit but not an evil person.

I'm sorry. God, am I sorry. I'm so sorry, so pathetic, but I *am* sorry.

I can still hear the voices in the crowd outside the hotel.

The paramedics roll me between two police cars and toward a waiting EMS truck, the meat wagon. The gurney bumps something, and I realize how absurd it is to be careful when you're carrying a dead body.

"Can't somebody help me?" I say, though I know the voice is only in my mind, whatever and wherever that is. But I can't stop pleading anyway. I won't give up, won't quit. Not *ever*. I won't go quietly.

"Somebody help me . . .

"Somebody, please . . .

"I'm sorry for all my sins, for everything I did."

Then a black woman leans in close, really close to my face, closer than I would ever get to a dead person. She shines a tiny flashlight into my eyes, and God do I want to blink—I'd do anything in the world to blink.

But I don't blink.

"Somebody, please help," I *don't* say again.

And then the woman steps away from me, and I see that she's an EMS doctor.

Suddenly, she yells in a clear voice, "This one is still alive!"

And I hope, I pray to God, that she's right.

"She's alive! This woman is alive! She just winked at me."

Author's Note

WHAT YOU JUST READ is the nightmare of anybody who believes in an afterlife. Obviously the story is an allegory about the horrors of an eternity in Hell. Like all of us, Kristin has made mistakes in her life, and in the book, she gets a second chance.

If you have questions or want to comment on *You've Been Warned*, please visit www.jamespatterson.com.

About the Authors

JAMES PATTERSON is one of the best-known and bestselling writers of all time. He is the author of the two top-selling new detective series of the past decade: the Alex Cross novels and the Woman's Murder Club series. He has written many other #1 bestsellers including *Step on a Crack, Suzanne's Diary for Nicholas, Lifeguard, Honeymoon, Beach Road,* and *Judge & Jury*. He lives in Florida.

HOWARD ROUGHAN is the author of *The Up and Comer* and *The Promise of a Lie,* and the coauthor, with James Patterson, of the #1 bestsellers *Honeymoon* and *You've Been Warned*. He lives in Connecticut with his wife and son.

THE NOVELS OF JAMES PATTERSON

Featuring Alex Cross

Double Cross
Cross
Mary, Mary
London Bridges
The Big Bad Wolf
Four Blind Mice
Violets Are Blue
Roses Are Red
Pop Goes the Weasel
Cat & Mouse
Jack & Jill
Kiss the Girls
Along Came a Spider

The Women's Murder Club

7th Heaven (coauthor Maxine Paetro)
The 6th Target (Maxine Paetro)
The 5th Horseman (Maxine Paetro)
4th of July (Maxine Paetro)
3rd Degree (Andrew Gross)
2nd Chance (Andrew Gross)
1st to Die

The James Patterson Pageturners

The Dangerous Days of Daniel X
(coauthor Michael Ledwidge)
The Final Warning: A Maximum Ride Novel
Saving the World and Other Extreme Sports:
A Maximum Ride Novel
Maximum Ride: School's Out—Forever
Maximum Ride: The Angel Experiment

Other Books

Sail (coauthor Howard Roughan)
Sundays at Tiffany's (Gabrielle Charbonnet)
You've Been Warned (Howard Roughan)
The Quickie (Michael Ledwidge)
Step on a Crack (Michael Ledwidge)
Judge & Jury (Andrew Gross)
Beach Road (Peter de Jonge)
Lifeguard (Andrew Gross)
Honeymoon (Howard Roughan)
santaKid
Sam's Letters to Jennifer
The Lake House
The Jester (Andrew Gross)
The Beach House (Peter de Jonge)
Suzanne's Diary for Nicholas
Cradle and All
When the Wind Blows
Miracle on the 17th Green (Peter de Jonge)
Hide & Seek
The Midnight Club
Black Friday (originally published as *Black Market*)
See How They Run (originally published as *The Jericho Commandment*)
Season of the Machete
The Thomas Berryman Number

The true story of one
family's courage,
heartbreak, and triumph.

Please turn this page
for a preview of

~

Against Medical Advice

BY JAMES PATTERSON

~

Available in hardcover

Preface

"ONE MORNING IN MARCH of 1989, I woke up as a normal five-year-old boy. By that afternoon I had an irresistible urge to shake my head, continually, and the course of my life changed in ways few people have ever seen before or could begin to understand.

"Before long, my body became an explosive, volatile, and unpredictable force with a mind and personality of its own. It jerked and twisted, bent in half, and gyrated without warning until I was almost always in motion.

"I bit down on my teeth until I actually broke them and howled in pain because of the exposed nerves.

"I twisted my back around with such force that I tore muscle tissue and had to be put to sleep at a hospital to stop doing it.

"My mind fed me thoughts so frightening I couldn't even talk about them to my parents.

"It didn't take long before I thought of myself as the oddest person in my town. I felt like a boy on the end of a puppeteer's string. What made it even worse was knowing that I was also the puppeteer."

*   *   *

Those are the words of Cory Friedman and what follows is his story, as told by his father, Hal, and a family friend, the author James Patterson.

In 1975, Patterson and Hal Friedman met for the first time in New York City, at the J. Walter Thompson Advertising Agency, where they were writers. They could hardly imagine then that more than thirty years later they would collaborate on a heart-wrenching nonfiction book about one of their sons.

Once a written account of Cory Friedman's life was drafted, they realized that it was not only a remarkable story, but one that had to be told because it would give hope to many people.

Thirteen doctors and *sixty* potent medicines after Cory's first traumatic head shakes, his complex combination of Tourette's syndrome, obsessive-compulsive disorder, and anxiety disorder was still unchecked.

Finally, when all of Cory's doctors, their advice, and their medicines had proven ineffective, an "intervention" was attempted that was as daring as anything that had preceded it, maybe even more so.

The events recounted here take place over what seemed like an endless period covering Cory's life from age five to twenty. The story is narrated in his voice because it is Cory's story, and because this is the most truthful and powerful way to tell it.

The names of friends, doctors, and medical institutions that are mentioned have been changed to protect privacy, and also because not all of them are presented in a favorable light.

A few doctors were remarkable advocates for Cory, bringing light and hope into his darkest hours. They know who they are, and so does Cory.

The harrowing events portrayed in this story have been reconstructed from Cory's own accounts, family observations over his lifetime, and detailed medical diaries kept by his mother throughout the period.

Hal Friedman
James Patterson

Part One

A LOST CHILDHOOD

At the Edge of Madness

Chapter 1

I'M SEVENTEEN YEARS OLD and lying like a sodden lump in the backseat of our family car, being transported to a place that treats crazy people.

This is an exceptional event, even for me. I know that my brain causes unusual problems that no one has been able to help, but being insane isn't one of them.

How and why I've gotten to this point is complicated, but the main reason I'm here is more immediate. The only escape I've found from my body is the calmness that a great amount of alcohol gives me.

Now this self-medication has become a life-threatening danger that I cannot fix by myself. The doctors at the place I'm going to have promised they can help me. I've heard that one before.

After a trip of about an hour, I see a sign in front of the large brick building that says NYU Psychiatric Hospital. In a split second the reality of what's happening is becoming very real and very scary.

"Why does it say that?" I call from the backseat, my heart suddenly pounding.

"Don't worry about the sign," my mother says to calm my rising panic. "They treat all different kinds of problems here, Cory."

Dad looks as worried as I am, but he says softly, "Let's not deal with this now, okay?"

Not deal with going to a hospital for psychos? Sure, no problem. What can my father be thinking?

Inside the main entrance, I walk into a very crowded, somewhat noisy waiting room. Being on view always makes me uneasy, so as soon as I start to walk, my feet need to perform a triple hop, three quick steps only inches apart, which throws me off balance.

I have to do this in order to satisfy a tension that is building up in my legs and can't be released in any other way. Sometimes this trips me up so much that I go flying to the ground.

I do the triple hop a few more times before reaching out for the safety of one of the empty waiting-room chairs.

Welcome to my fun house, folks.

Chapter 2

MANY OF THE PEOPLE in the waiting area are still staring at me as my right hand shoots up in the air with the middle finger extended. *Oh boy, here we go,* I think. Giving people the bird is another one of my involuntary movements, called tics, that pop up exactly when they shouldn't. Try telling people that one's not deliberate.

Another middle-finger salute. *Hi, everybody!*

For a moment I think about the new medicines I'm taking, which are, as usual, not doing their job. Wellbutrin for depression, Tenex to keep me calm, Topamax as an "experiment" to see if a seizure medicine will help. So far I've been on fifty or sixty different medicines that haven't helped—and a few of them can become deadly when washed down with Jack Daniel's.

Psychiatric hospital. A place for insane people, I'm thinking.

I know I'm not insane, even though the things I do make me look that way. But I do have a fear that I can think myself insane, and being in this place could push me over the edge. Going insane is probably my worst fear. If it happens I won't know what or where reality is. To me, that's the ultimate isolation—to be separated from my own mind.

Eventually a receptionist calls my name and then starts asking me strange, bewildering questions. One of my eyes begins to twitch rapidly, and my tongue jumps out of my mouth like a snake.

Occasionally I make a loud grunting sound like I've been punched hard in the stomach. Usually my tics come one at a time, but today they're arriving in clusters of three and four, probably due to the stress.

I once told my parents that they couldn't live through a single day with what I go through *all the time,* and that was when I was *a lot better* than I am now.

It takes another hour or so for my parents to be interviewed by a doctor. When they come out, I can see that my mother has been crying. My father looks exhausted and edgy.

When it's my turn with the doctor, I can't stop myself from shooting him the bird, too. The guy is good about it. He totally ignores it. He's young and gentle and pretty much puts me at ease.

"I drink more than I should at night," I tell him, skipping the part about almost burning down my parents' house when I passed out on the couch with a lit cigarette. "I guess I like to get a little tipsy."

This is the understatement of the year. *Tipsy* is my code word for totally wasted.

The doctor gives me a complete physical, and when it's over he says I'm as healthy as anyone he's seen, which strikes me as very funny.

"So I guess I can go now?" I joke, punctuated by an involuntary tongue thrust.

"Yeah, right."

Later, back in the waiting area, a male attendant approaches us and asks for any medicines we might have brought.

"What do you mean?" my father asks.

"He needs these," my mother cautions, taking out a large plastic bag crammed with pill bottles.

"The doctors will take care of that," the attendant answers. "Give them over."

Mom reluctantly turns over the stash.

A while later, a female nurse approaches and leads the three of us deep into the rear of the building.

Everything is a lot different here. It's darker and there aren't any people around. The walls are dirty and cracked. It's a spooky place.

I fight off a real bad feeling that I'm going somewhere I won't be able to handle.

Eventually we stop in front of a massive door with a sign that says Juvenile Psychiatric Ward D.

Mental kids, I think.

"That's not me," I snap, pointing to the sign. "Mom, you know I'm not crazy."

The nurse says, "We get all kinds of people here," as though arriving at an insane asylum is an ordinary event in anybody's life.

"You're here for your drinking," Mom adds. "They know that, Cory."

"It doesn't say that on the signs."

The nurse takes a large metal key out of her jacket pocket, and I freeze at the sight of it. I've never been in a hospital where the doors have to be locked. The reason is suddenly obvious. You don't lock doors to keep people *out*. You lock doors to keep them *in*.

Chapter 3

DAD GETS IT, TOO. He and I exchange fearful glances, and he lightly touches my arm.

The door opens as if it weighs a thousand pounds. When I refuse to move, my father holds onto my arm tightly and guides me into the ward, which turns out to be another disappointing surprise. The main corridor is small, maybe fifty feet long before it goes at a right angle to *somewhere*. There are no nurses, doctors, or equipment around, not like any other hospital I've been in.

Three boys are standing together at the end of the hall. They stare at me and whisper to one another. Then they disappear.

A man hunched over a computer in a small office turns out to be the ward supervisor. He's dressed in very casual clothes, not looking like a doctor.

He keeps working for a while, and when he finally turns to us, I notice that his eyes are unfocused. He seems to be either stoned or a little retarded. If I didn't know who he was, I'd guess he was a patient. Or should be.

After going over my papers, he leads the three of us

farther into the ward. There are small offices on either side of the main corridor. One of them is for dispensing medicine and has metal bars over the opening.

We take a sharp right turn in the corridor. All of the patients' rooms are in this area, on both sides. There's also a common area with a TV playing, but no one is watching it.

"How many kids are here?" I ask.

"Right now, eleven. Never more than fifteen. That's a hospital rule."

As we pass by the rooms, I count about eight kids and have no idea where the rest are hiding. All are teenagers, none as old as I am.

The three boys I saw before appear again at the end of this corridor. As I get nearer, they split up and walk past me, deadly serious. This is not a bunch I want to be around when the lights go out. That especially includes the supervisor.

I'm getting more uncomfortable by the second. My skin is oozing a cold sweat. Hop. Hop. Hop.

I can't do this. I'm ticcing like crazy now.

In a moment we come to a large sign on the wall with rules printed in thick black letters.

NO TWO IN A ROOM

DOORS MUST REMAIN OPEN AT ALL TIMES

ALL ARTICLES IN THE PATIENT'S POSSESSION UPON ADMISSION WILL BE CONFISCATED

PERMISSION REQUIRED TO LEAVE PREMISES AT ALL TIMES

NO STANDING ON WINDOWSILLS

NO STANDING ON UPPER BUNKS

I wonder about this last one, then look up at the ceiling

and understand. The entire area is covered with a metal grating. The openings in the grid are too small to put your hand through. *This whole ward is a giant cage.*

My heart is pounding, as if it wants to jump right out of my chest and die on the hospital floor. How bad must this place be if people have tried getting out through the ceiling?

"I'm not staying here!" I shout to my parents. "Don't you understand? I can't do this."

I back away, then turn and start for the main door, the only way out.

I want to run but hold myself in check so I won't look like I'm trying to escape and get whoever else is around to come chasing after me.

"I'm not like these people," I call back to my father.

My sudden decision throws my parents into confusion. I think coming to a place that looks like this is as much of a shock for them as it is for me.

"I'm not crazy! This place will *make* me crazy."

My father's expression changes slightly, and I can see in it a small ray of hope. He seems sympathetic yet angry at me at the same time, and I can't read which emotion is winning.

"You can't give up without trying," he says finally. "Give it time to work out."

"I'm *leaving;* didn't you hear me?"

"What choice do you have? Think about it. This isn't your choice anymore."

This message sends me into a rage. I'm spinning out of control. I'll crash my way out if I have to.

I quickly rush to the door and stop when I see that

there's another golden rule on it, etched on a bronze plate. This one stops me cold.

NO ONE PERMITTED OUTSIDE AFTER 6 PM

My watch says seven twenty. We've already been in this so-called hospital for over three hours.

I try the door anyway. It doesn't move, not even a jiggle. You need a key from this side, too.

My anxiety spikes way past panic. If they lock me up, my life will be over. I'll die of fear. People can die of fear. I've read about it.

"Take a few deep breaths and try to calm down," my mother says when she catches up to me. "I know you're scared, Cory. We'll work something out. We always do."

"I promise I'll stop drinking on my own," I plead, my voice cracking with emotion. I'm completely helpless, dependent on her — as usual. "I swear it. Please, Mom, I know I can do it on my own. *Don't make me stay!*"

Chapter 4

IT'S A FEW MINUTES after the supervisor left us alone to talk, and we're back with him in his small office. My father is having a really hard time deciding what to do. He's usually fast with decisions, but this one is giving him trouble.

Finally, he takes a breath and delivers the words I've been praying for. "We don't think this is what we need for our son after all. We had a different idea of the hospital before we came."

I'm joyous inside. My father has done a complete about-face and is now going to fight for me. I want to hug him.

Unbelievably, the supervisor isn't taking my father seriously. He shakes his head, like he doesn't care what my dad just said.

"I'd appreciate you letting us out," my father announces again.

He has to say it a third time before it seems to sink in with the guy.

"It's not possible for Cory to leave," the supervisor reports without any emotion. "Once a patient is admitted to the ward, New York State requires a minimum seventy-two hour stay. It's the law."

"But we're *not* admitting him," my father explains. "We're going to leave right now, *before* he's admitted."

"He's already admitted," the man says more strongly. "It happened when he came through that door. Seventy-two hours, no exceptions," he adds after delivering what to him are just simple facts.

To me the number of hours—seventy-two—is like a death sentence to be executed in slow motion.

"I want to speak to the hospital administrator," my father barks, and he stands up. When the supervisor still doesn't react, he says, "Let me put it another way. I *demand* to speak to the administrator."

The supervisor thinks about it, then shrugs and picks up his phone. In a minute he hands the receiver to my dad.

My mother and I look at each other nervously. Everything is riding on the next conversation.

My father takes the phone and tells the administrator what's going on. Then he listens for a long time, and my mother and I don't know what's being said.

"There has to be a way," he says finally, obviously very frustrated. "What if someone came here by mistake, like we have?"

The debate continues, and he's beginning to lose his temper, which isn't like him.

"Even a criminal can post bond and get out of jail. What do you want me to do, call a lawyer?"

My father keeps going at the administrator. It seems hopeless, then, all at once, he stops talking. "Yes, I understand. Thank you. I will." He hangs up and turns to us. "Maybe" is all he says.

Mom and I are both surprised when we hear who he's calling next.

"Dr. Ferrise! Thank God you picked up."

Ferrise is my current therapist. It's an absolute stroke of luck that he has answered his phone this late at night. We usually get his message machine.

"We have an emergency here, and you're our only hope," my father continues.

The two of them talk for a few more minutes as he explains the situation.

After a while he lets out a deep breath.

"Say it just like that?" he asks. "Exactly that way?" He nods to us, then thanks Dr. Ferrise and hangs up.

My father turns to the supervisor and announces defiantly to him, "I request the release of my son AMA."

The man cocks his head suspiciously but doesn't respond verbally. Not a word.

My father repeats the special code letters, this time as an order. "We are leaving the hospital with our son AMA. I'm told you understand what that means."

In a moment, the supervisor nods reluctantly, then gets on the phone again.

While he's talking to someone high up, my father explains, "AMA is an acronym for against medical advice. It's a legal code that allows the hospital to go around the law. It means that we understand the hospital advises against it, and it shifts responsibility to us, the parents, and our therapist. It lets the hospital off the hook in case a patient . . , harms himself or something."

"You know I wouldn't do that," I reply, to reinforce his decision.

"It's the only way we have a chance of getting you out of here."

"And what if we never learned about AMA?" my mother asks. "Or if Ferrise wasn't around or didn't pick up?"

My father shakes his head. "We were lucky. Very lucky."

I study my father's face after he finishes. He looks older than I've ever seen him. He's worn out. It's been as long a day for him as for me.

"Sorry, Dad."

He nods, but isn't happy. "You know that we haven't fixed what we came here for."

It's not a question.

A long time later, the nightmare is finally ending. The supervisor is still waiting for whatever approvals he needs. My breathing has almost returned to normal.

Eventually someone comes into the ward with papers and the required signatures, and the supervisor gets his key, and the thousand-pound door swings open again.

It's been five hours since we entered the hospital. I walk out the front door without looking back.

The ride home to New Jersey is silent. No one has the energy to say anything, and nothing we can talk about seems important compared to what's just happened.

My mother lets me smoke a cigarette, then a second one, and after that I fall asleep. In an hour or so, they wake me in New Jersey and I drag myself into our darkened house.

"I really mean it, Mom. I'm going to quit drinking," I tell her before going to bed. "I know I can do it."

I'm not lying. I really believe I can.

It's the middle of the week, and my resolve lasts until Friday night, when my body is again driving me crazy. After my parents go to bed, I sneak down to the basement and chug five or six big swallows from a bottle of vodka my father thought he'd hidden from me. In a short time the bottle is only half full.

I fall asleep with my head reeling. Images of the psychiatric ward are getting hazier. I have a dim awareness that despite my honest desire to change, my absolute need to change, I won't be able to.

Something else is going to have to happen. And happen soon.